A House with no Angels

A House with no Angels

Muli Amaye

ISBN 9780946745296
Crocus

Skilfully crafted and impossible to put down. A tale of three generations of a Nigerian family based in Manchester from the 1940s onwards, as told by grandmother, daughter and granddaughter. Love, betrayal, Pan-Africanism, humour. Read and enjoy!

Hakim Adi, Professor of Pan-Africanism and the African Diaspora.

"A multi-generational story of arrivals and departures – Nigeria and England - providing an interesting intertwining of postcolonial personalities, relationships and women's lives and an intriguing setting for ordinary women's engagement with the 1945 Fifth pan-African Congress in Manchester.

Rhoda Reddock, Professor of Gender, Social Change and Development

History is heroic, haphazard even humorous because it is reliant on memory. This novel evokes memories so real the reader is swept into a past so important for the continent.

SuAndi

First published in 2019 by Crocus

Crocus books are published by Commonword, 3 Planetree House, 21-31 Oldham Street, Manchester, M1 1JG

A CIP catalogue for this book is available from the British Library.

admin@cultureword.org.uk

Crocus books are distributed by Turnaround Publisher Services Ltd, Unit 3, Olympia Trading Estate, Coburg Rd, Wood Green, London N22 6TZ UK

Cover design by tymedesign
Printed by biddles.co.uk

CROCUS

Supported using public funding by
**ARTS COUNCIL
ENGLAND**

Acknowledgements

Dedicated to all the women who laid the path for us to walk a little easier.

Thank you to Graham Mort at Lancaster University, who supervised and supported me and provoked me into writing better than I thought I could.

Also, to Commonword Advanced Novelist Group who took me into the fold and gave me a space and encouragement to explore diasporic boundaries.

I'm grateful to all my friends who listened to me mapping out this book, asked questions, made suggestions and introduced me to people who could help. To my brother, Sigma, who assisted with names and places in Nigeria. Also, to the other members of my family who critiqued me into doing better. To my daughter, Mel, who was part of the struggle. And most especially to my son, Simon, who expected nothing less than completion.

Final thanks go to my late father, Samuel Diden Yalaju-Amaye who claimed me and to my mother, Dorothy Steadman, who kept me.

Crocus acknowledges the support of The Research & Publication Fund Committee at The University of the West Indies, St. Augustine, Trinidad, which has assisted in the publication of this work.

Elizabeth

I'm half way round the lake at Chorlton Water Park. It's what I do on Monday afternoons. I listen to the birds, sit on this bench and watch the ducks. Sometimes there's a heron that stands on the left side of the lake. Damn, I can hear a magpie behind me, but if I don't turn around I won't see it and it won't be bad luck.

Dad used to take me to the park when I was small. The lake there wasn't wild like this one, though. A few orderly ducks and a couple of swans. Sometimes Dad pretended there was a ship for us to get on.

My phone is ringing. It isn't supposed to. This is my time. It's Kutes, and she isn't saying very much, just that Ola's crying and I'd better go home and see what's wrong with him. As usual, she doesn't say his name. She says 'your brother'.

I don't want to go home. I have things to think about. Kutes is one of them. I need a strategy, apparently. To negotiate the teenage hormones and create balance. Bollocks. I need to get away from her. It's too bloody stressful. How am I supposed to control a seventeen year old who happens to be stunning and knows it and has worked out that guys will do anything she asks? I didn't bring her up like that. Maybe Dia's right and she's searching for her father figure. Maybe that's why she's seeing a man who is more than twice her age and looks it and is old and controlling, did I mention that he's old? For fuck's sake. Breathe. She'll grow out of it. As long as she doesn't get knocked up.

'What Mum?'

'Of course I'm on my way.'

God, she's like my mother sometimes. What can be so bloody important that I must leave right now? Oh, great, not happy with just letting me know you're there Mr Magpie, you have to prance around in front of me. Cheers for that. I might as well go now because my whole afternoon has gone to shit. It couldn't be any worse.

Except that obviously it can be, because Dia won't be coming round for dinner. She was a right bitch last night. There's no need for it. I'm not dumping her, for god's sake. And I'm not literally moving back home. Mum's house is split into apartments, flats. It's not like I'm going back to live with her. Why the hell did Kutes ring and what the fuck's wrong with Ola?

1

There are more red traffic lights than green between the water park and home so by the time I arrive I know it isn't going to be good news. I like this house. My lavender plants need watering. I'm not sure I want to leave here.

The hallway smells of cranberry juice. Ocean Spray. The lilies on the hall table are shedding their pollen and their perfume makes me think of magic potions. My skin looks yellow and pinched. It should be shining with the cold air and the walk I've just had. And why is there a greasy mark in the corner of the mirror, I know I cleaned it properly.

'I've gotta be in work soon. Are you taking me still?'

She's made a mess on my cream rug.

'Do your homework upstairs, please. You've got a desk in your room so why are you sprawled out on my floor? I hope you're going to get changed.'

Her eyes don't leave the television.

'Did you hear me?'

Nothing.

'Has Ola been down? Have you spoken to him?'

Of course, there's still no response. It's like I don't exist.

Upstairs it's all quiet so there can't be that much wrong. Nothing compared to the fact that Dia might be leaving me, that Kutes is dating a man old enough to be her father and that she's made a mess on my rug. There's no need for more drama, really, but why shouldn't Ola get in on it?

I'm going to have to repaint this bannister before we leave. Just refresh the white paint. I don't want the tenants to paint anything. God, can you imagine, bright pinks and lime greens.

'What's wrong Ola? Has something happened to you?'

'Papa's gone.'

His head's buried in his arms and it's hard to make out what he's saying.

'Gone where? What do you mean gone? Who says he's gone? I don't know what you mean.' I can hear my voice rising.

He's moved his arm now. He hasn't had a shave. When he rubs his cheek like that it sounds like crumbling crisps. He looks too wide for the bed. Too long. His feet are almost touching the wall. I suppose it's more of a kid's room than for a grown man, but it's not like I invited him. He just turned up.

'Papa's dead. He's gone. Tosan rang me...'

'That can't be right. How can he be dead?'

Am I shouting?

My dad's dead.

Bad things shouldn't happen on the tenth. I can hear Ola crying, but I don't feel anything. Okay, I knew dad was ill, but not that ill. It doesn't make sense. I pat Ola's leg. It can't be true. Kutes is shouting. Ola's looking at me. His eyes are red and swollen and ugly. He gets hold of my hand with his own wet one and I don't know if it's tears or snot but I don't want it touching me.

Four, six, two to the bathroom. Wash and rinse four times, dry, wash and rinse twice more, dry. Two, two, then down the stairs in thirteen. To the front door, four.

'I'll be in the car. Hurry up. And take all that mess upstairs.'

I'm aware that I'm fiddling. The rear-view mirror, the wing mirrors, the pile of toffee papers that are on the dashboard. It's obvious that something bad could happen. I haven't been paying attention.

Kutes

jeez me mum never stops moan moan moan she needs to get a grip at least I rang her whats her problem anyways im gonna get changed whats wrong wiv these jeans an I have to wear me vest top cos ive gotta put me work tshirt on over it an there aint no way that skanky tops touchin me skin its gross an anyways she looks a right mess them jeans were in fashion mebbe 60 years ago an that hippy top all floaty an loose like yeah man an it aint like shes fat or summat so theres no need to wear baggy shit an I don't know why she scrapes her hair back like shes some kind of chav why dunt she put the friggin straightners on it an make herself look nice an she stands there with them goggle eyes like I just sicked up on the floor she needs to deal wiv her random brother innit instead of goin on at me for nothing she gets on me tits least I was doin me homework so what if I was watchin tele I swear down I cant wait to move to me nans house so I dont have to see her everyday then I cud bring carls over or Carly as Mum insists on calling her whenever I want itll be proper cool an that

Ade

So, my husband has gone. Before I lifted the telephone to my ear and before Funmi greeted me I sensed that something had happened. I do not know how many hours I have been sitting in this chair but my body is stiff. My room looks strange to me, as though I have just entered somewhere I do not know. James is dead. He is gone. If it had not been for that man, sha! But what am I saying? Did he force me to come to this place?

The journey-o! How I survived it I do not know. When we arrived in Lagos port I thought I would pass out. The smell! Aiy-aiy-aiy! The ship was so large. I had never seen anything so big in my life. But of course I was young and excited. I was more concerned with looking over my shoulder to make sure that I had not been followed. I do not think I shed one tear at the thought of leaving my home.

It was not as difficult as we thought it would be for me to slip into James's car at the edge of the village. When Funmi and I reach the Iroko tree, the women's tree, I look up. It is as though the moon is impaled on its highest branch. Earlier the children were playing, as they do at full moon, placing broken chalk and china around each other to create moon-babies that litter the floor. I grip Funmi's hand, suddenly frightened.

'What if he does not turn up? What will I do? I will die.'

'Sistah, I beg, you do not need to do this. It will be well. Mama will understand.'

'But Funmi, I love him. Can you not be happy for me?'

'But, sistah, he is so old?'

'What do you mean? He is twenty-five. Just eight years more than me.'

'Yes, eight. What will his job be in England? Do you think he can look after you? Will he still drive for his government?'

I try to let go of her hand, but she grips me tight. The air is still, thick. The scent of evening rides on top of it. Saturating my senses. Pepper soup is mixed with charcoal and the village latrines. The river is glinting as the moon whispers its secrets in a thousand voices to its ebb and flow.

Funmi begins to cry, quietly. We hear the thrum-thrum of the car's engine as it loops around the village. My heart leaps and my insides tighten and I know I am doing the right thing. The headlights create shadows of us that reach up into the branches. Stretching for the moon. We hide behind the tree. Just in case it is my papa returning. James drives over the thick, knobbled roots and pulls up right beside us.

'Ade, hurry up. I saw you. Come on, quick.'

'I'm coming. I'm coming.'

I turn to Funmi. I cannot see her but I can feel her. Her fear is trying to hold on to me. To stop me from leaving.

'Remember, Funmi, you do not know anything. Promise me again that you will not tell. Promise me.'

In the back of my mind I know that I am sentencing her. When Papa returns he will beat her. If Mama has not banished her before then. Her own mama, my aunty, will take pleasure in our downfall. But there is nothing I can do. I must go.

I climb into the backseat. The car smells of leather and tobacco. It smells of James. He switches off the headlights and we drive away with the moon riding on the bonnet. I dare to look up one more time. I think I can make out Funmi. She is standing, her hand over her mouth as though to stop herself shouting out. Mud houses and the concrete school shimmer, like a mirage in the desert. I do not cry.

When we have travelled for some time, James says, 'Ade, sit up now and look like somebody.'

I sit as I have seen Papa sit many times in the back of that big, black car. I would like to ride up front with James, but I do not know how to ask him. Instead I breathe him in until I feel dizzy with the fumes.

'Tell me again, James, where will we live?'

'I've told you half a dozen times. I need to concentrate. Do you want us to be ambushed?'

Of course I did not. But at that time I could not imagine who would want to ambush us. Especially if we were in a white man's car. Belonging to the Foreign Office. I was too young to understand. But I did not wish to irritate James. We were going on an adventure. We were starting our new life. We would marry and have our baby and live in James's England. I lay my head on my luggage and slept.

Elizabeth

When we set off, I have to readjust the mirrors because I can't see a thing. Kutes is looking at me. I can feel it. The radio front flicks out at one side and I almost ram it into place and turn the volume up loud. She's still looking at me.

It's 4.45 and it's rush hour and I don't want to be driving. When I get to the end of the street nineteen cars pass before I can pull out. Kutes is still looking at me, she has that pout on her face that I want to slap off. Dia says she'll grow out of it.

'Grandad's dead,' I shout over Luther Van Dross. Kutes turns down the radio and looks sideways at me. Our eyes meet for the first time in I don't know how long and she quickly looks away.

'I'll have to drop you at the corner, okay? I need to get back.'

'Shit, mum, are you okay?'

'Course I am. What do you mean? I've got to get back. I've got to find out what happened. I don't think Ola's okay.'

The traffic's so heavy; I've counted to seven hundred and two by the time we get on to Regent Road. I can do that. Have a conversation, listen to the radio and still keep the count.

'You can drop me here. Thanks. You can turn down there then, can't you? It'll be quicker for me to walk from here anyways.'

I take a sharp left before the Urban Splash bubble. The bubble appeared a few years ago, it's supposed to be a funky office or something. A silver sphere in the middle of original, redbrick warehouses and an old-fashioned railway bridge. It's wrong. Everything's wrong. A pain is starting over my left eye and I need to be at home. Kutes is getting out of the car and saying something to me and I can't work out what and I've lost my count because I have to ask her to repeat it.

Hot chocolate. Ola loves hot chocolate so I boil the kettle. I wash, dry and put away the plate, mug and knife that Kutes has left. I have to wipe all the surfaces, even though I know she's only had a sandwich. There are crumbs and slops of mayonnaise everywhere. The kettle boils and I make the drink and take it upstairs. I don't count. There's no point. It's too late. Ola's on his back staring at the ceiling.

'I brought you a drink. You should have something. Here. Sit up. It's chocolate.'

He doesn't act like he's heard me so I set it down on the little table next to his bed. The room's tiny. When he turned up on my doorstep eight months ago with one small suitcase, it wasn't a problem for me to clear the box room and fit him in here. Of course, I didn't know him when he arrived. The last time I'd seen him he was about ten years old. He had short pants and a check shirt that was buttoned up wrong and he was so skinny. But when I opened the door to him here he was a man and I didn't know him. I should have. Even if he's only half a brother.

His laptop's open on the table where I've put the drink and I watch the zigzag lines floating around the black screen. It's very soothing.

'Are you going to drink your hot chocolate?'

Still no response. The combi wardrobe's so bursting with clothes the door won't close and on the chair in front of it there's a pile of neatly folded jeans, some still with TK Maxx tags on them. I start to count them while I wait for Ola to say something. I've got to nine when I feel him move but I carry on to the top of the pile. Thirteen. I have to count down again.

'What happened, Ola? I don't understand.'

He sits up and takes hold of my hand, which makes me cry. He puts his arm around me and pulls me into his shoulder.

'I don't know. I don't know what happened. Tosan rang me. My sister rang me. I'll phone her back later. When she gets home, I'll phone back.'

We sit like that for a few minutes until I push myself away from him.

'Drink your hot chocolate, it'll get cold. I need to make dinner.'

Kutes

Shit cant believe me grandads snuffed it but it aint surprisin is it really cos it aint like he was young or summat but that means me nan aint young an she might snuff it an that would be like really shit cos then I'd have to deal with me mum on me own an she's gonna be bad enough about me grandad an she dint even know him proper an it aint like he was all that is it cos from what me nan says I reckon he was a right bastard the way he like got off an left her an that an she goes on like he was always right an shit an there aint no way I would've well ditched him an changed the locks an then hes like livin in me nans country an droppin more kids an shit an I bet he had a proper young wife the creep Emre aint like that if he was married to me an we were like livin in Cyprus yeah he wouldnt like get off an move here an leave me there thatd be like mad innit damn that guys fine an he's lookin at me I cant wait to tell carls no way is he shoutin at me like he thinks I'm gonna stop an chat as if shit I shunt be lookin if Im with Emre I keep forgettin oh well I cant help me eyes its not like I told them to look I hope me shift goes quick I hate workin I hope Im on the tills cos I aint picking up all the crap off the floor its like people think theres servants in clothes shops innit the way they pick things up an then dash em on the floor it aint fair that Ive gotta work an if me mums carryin on like that there aint no way shes gonna come an get me howm I gonna get home an I aint got any credit to ring her shit

Ade

Only once did I sense James's fear. When we arrived in Lagos, close to the port, another car, the same kind, pulled up alongside. The sun had begun to rise and push the moon away. The darkness ahead of us was turning into distinct shapes. Large, bulky shapes. I could see a busy bustle of people, flashes of reds and greens as lantern light caught a trouser or shirt. James told me to keep smiling, to greet the other man as though I was used to it. His fear made my whole body prickle. I did not want to return to my village and face Mama. He took himself to one side with the man and they talked. James's hands were moving quick-quick, the way they did when he was nervous. He handed the keys to the other man and shook his hand. When he returned to me he said, 'Don't worry Ade, I covered for you.' Killing two birds with one stone is what James said to him. Killing two birds with one stone-o. He lied so easily. But of course I did not know back then. He was protecting me.

Hei! the smell. I never imagined the port would smell of rotting vegetables. Nobody else seemed to notice but my stomach did not allow me to ignore it and I leaned up against the car while I vomited. James stroked my back and handed me his handkerchief. It smelled of cologne. Holding it against my nose I was able to calm my insides. There were so many people pushing, shouting. It was like a whole new world. I gazed around as white people called to porters and carriers,

'You, hey, you there, carry this, carry that, help here, help there.'

Beside me James sucked his teeth and spit on the floor, 'first class' he muttered.

I did not know what he meant until we walked up the wooden plank, holding on to the thick rope that swayed each time a new person grabbed hold of it. The steward looked at our papers and pointed to the left. The white people in front of us went in the other direction. James walked ahead of me down a narrow corridor that was lit intermittently with wall lanterns. Wooden doors on each side had numbers painted in black. The lower we walked the smaller the doors seemed and they were much closer together. It was too dark, as though we were going down to the bottom of the sea. We stopped outside one of the doors and James opened it. I smelled mould. Like wrappers left damp in the corner of a room.

I held on to James's arm. My stomach was revolting at the unaccustomed movement beneath my feet.

'I'm scared. Where will you be? Can we not stay together?'

Of course we could not do so. It would not have been correct. James wrapped his arms around me. He pressed his sunburned lips on the side of my neck. Their roughness was like the bark on a tree. I clung to him. I cried.

'Shhhh! It's okay, picken. Don't cry, Ade. Shhhhh!'

I could not stand the thought of him leaving me in that dungeon of a ship. When I calmed down he held the paper map under the lantern and pointed out where his own cabin was.

'See Ade, I am not so far away from you. Just around that corner and up one deck.'

It seemed like a whole world away.

It was hard to imagine that only nine weeks before I had been carefree. When I realised that my monthly had not arrived as usual, I felt only excitement. Of course, we knew what it meant. Mama had told us about it. Funmi was scared. When James took me to the river, the part behind the schoolhouse, I told him immediately.

'James-o, we are having a baby.'

I was too silly to be nervous. I did not think.

'Oh my god! Ade, no. How did this happen?'

Two things amused me. One, that he said god, when he had told me many times god did not exist. Two, that he did not know how it had happened. Of course, I did not laugh.

'But James, does it not mean we can be together now? Will we not marry?'

I forced some tears into my eyes. Had I not read about gentlemen not coping well with a woman's tears in many of the books that the nuns made us read? James did not even look at my eyes. He was too busy standing and telling me about how he had to go and that he would speak to me the next tomorrow. For one week I did not see him and I thought I would go mad. For one week Funmi and I cried about what was happening. We planned how we could make it right. The shame would be too much for my family.

After one week James returned and signalled for me to meet him at the river. The water was low because of the dry season. The earth was parched and cracked and alive with beetles and ants. I sat high up amongst the bushes.

The dry air carries the sound of the young children singing their morning

11

prayers. The sun is cloaked in a haze that is unusual for this time of year. The red earth crumbles between my fingers and leaves a layer of dust over my palms. Blowing it away, I make a wish. I arrange my green wrapper prettily around my legs. James likes this one. Ever since I told him it makes his grey eyes change colour. He comes from behind and puts his arms around me. Although my belly is still flat, for a moment he cradles it in his hands. His arm catches the side of my breast and the slight pain I feel makes me smile. It makes it all real. I lean back against him. I am safe.

'Ade, we must arrange matters. I have spoken to the nuns in Lagos, you can go there until afterwards. Your parents do not need to know. We can say you are training with them or something. The nuns will take care of everything. It is not the first time this has happened.'

'You have done this before? But I thought you loved me. I thought this was special.'

Of course, James has not done this before. He is talking about other white men. About other village girls. Girls who do not know any better. Who do not have education. That is not me. I am not one of those girls.

'I would rather throw myself in this river. If you make me go I will tell Papa. He will kill you. If you try to leave me he will take you into the bush and you will disappear and nobody will know what happened.'

'Ade, don't say those things. You know I love you.'

'Your body will rot there and animals will tear you apart. And soldier ants will eat your eyes. You'll never be discovered. I swear, he'll do it. Nobody will ever know.'

'I don't believe you, Ade. He'd never do that. I work for the Government. You're just confused. Stop saying those things. I only want what's best for you.'

'He'll do it and then he will beat me. And I will be put out like aunty was and I will go mad. No decent man will ever touch me. And it will be your fault, James. All your fault.'

I did not believe any of the things I was saying, but I was desperate. How could I face Mama and tell her what I had done? What we had done. This time my tears were genuine. When I did not stop crying he promised me he would fix it. He would make everything okay. And he did. He arranged everything. My papers. My passport. It was fortunate that Papa was suddenly sent to work away and Mama became too distracted to notice what I was doing.

Whenever he could James came to our village and we went into the bush. He told me stories about his England. He explained about where we would live and what we would do. When I asked about the journey he told me the ship was like a big village. Eeh! My village never rolled around like this.

My cabin was shared with one other lady who was going to join her husband. Mrs Okorro. Regina. I remember her name because she told me it meant the queen. I am sure I must have her letters somewhere. I will look for them. If it had not been for her, I would have died right there on the ship. I did not think I would last the journey on that tiny bunk that was suspended from the wall. Vomiting. Too much vomiting. I was like a small child. I could barely lift my head. Mrs Okorro brought a bucket for me and emptied it regularly. As we rolled around on that ocean each sip of water she gave me was out before it even hit my stomach.

James came to see me every day. He knocked on the cabin door and Mrs Okorro opened it and stepped outside. I am sure she was relieved to get some fresh air. James placed his handkerchief over his nose and stood by my bunk briefly. I was delirious with sickness. My wrapper, soaked with the sweat of illness, clung to me. He patted me on my head, unheeding, moved back to the open door and waited for her to return so he could escape me. I did not care.

After one week of illness I began to feel better and was able to keep some dry food down. Mrs Okorro brought me water to bathe and stepped outside to give me some privacy. When the first cramp squeezed my belly I screamed. It took less than thirty minutes for my baby to be expelled from my body. The doctor arrived and took away the bucket and gave me a sedative. I dreamed of Mama. I dreamed I was at home.

When James next came to visit, Mrs Okorro did not leave the cabin as she had previously. It made it difficult for us to talk. But I could not complain about her. She was the one who held my hand while I cried. Not once did she berate me for what I had done.

When I finally dressed in my English clothes they dripped off me like rain from a banana leaf. I had to wear my wrapper while Mrs Okorro sewed my skirt in at the sides and showed me how to tuck in my blouse so that it did not look as though it was six sizes too big. She took me up to the deck where I breathed in the fresh air. The breeze was strong and made my whole body tingle after being wrapped in sickness for so long. I was too weak so we sat down in the blue and white striped deckchairs that lined the sides of the deck. On the other side, close to the rail, people were fanning themselves, talking and drinking from delicate glasses. I had

13

never seen so many white people in one place.

James was running around chat-chatting to every man who looked as though he was someone. The sea is calm he told me, patting my arm when he occasionally passed me by. Calm. Eh-heh! For a brief moment I worried about what I had done.

Elizabeth

Ola follows me downstairs and sits at the kitchen table sniffing. I have to cook but I can't remember what I'd planned to make. I did have a plan up on the fridge but Kutes and Dia laughed too much so I took it down. Now I have to remember what I want to make each day.

'Sistah, do you want me to help you?'

'Of course not. I cook every night.'

I feel like I'm in a movie and I should be swooning over the frigging sofa or something. Maybe that's what I should be doing. But then that doesn't make sense because my dad is-was-Ola's dad, so he would be in the same state. Except that he's a man so he'd have to show his grief in a different way. Shepherd's pie. That's what I'm supposed to be making. And cauliflower cheese.

'What are you saying, sistah? I can't hear you. Are you counting?'

'No. I'm thinking a bit out loud. Why would I be counting?'

On and on. It's obvious I'm not talking to him, I'm just trying to sort things out.

'Have you spoken to Tosan again? Did you manage to get her?'

'No, sistah, she has to travel from Warri to Benin. I will try later or she will call me.'

The pain in my head's getting worse. My dad's dead. Our dad's dead. But he hadn't been dying, he'd been ill. Ill and dying are not the same thing. What do you do next when your dad has died? How should I be feeling? I wonder what the modern equivalent of swooning is. Punching things? Running amok? That's a good word. But not really a death word. Maybe I'm supposed to be sitting down in the lounge with the curtains drawn and neighbours bringing food? That's how it used to be. I remember. The old lady across the road died. I was about nine. I'd never liked her. She had a strange face and would stand at her gate all the time. She tried to talk but her mouth dropped and dribbled and we made up stories about her. How she was a witch who cast spells on little kids she didn't like. When she died all the neighbours closed their curtains. I stood behind our hedge and watched them taking pans and cake tins to her family. Even Mum took a pan of stew. It went on for days. John Sinclair, who lived two doors down, said if we didn't close our curtains and take nice food she'd come and stare in our windows at night-time and give the evil eye to people who'd laughed at her and if they looked at her their face

15

would drop. He also said his mum had gone and seen her in the coffin. She was on the dining room table. Her face was proper, he said. Smooth and straight. And she had no toes. I wet the bed that night. On the day of her funeral we had to dress up in our best clothes and stand outside when the coffin came out. I stood behind my mum and closed my eyes.

Ola's putting the phone in my hand, I hadn't heard it ring. It's Dia and I say, 'My dad's dead' and she puts the phone down.

I only have time to fill the mop bucket before the doorbell rings. That's mainly because Ola is insisting on helping me and I don't need him to help, I need to mop. His incessant talking is making me feel like screaming at him, but I can't. His dad's just died.

I open the door to Dia. She has on her black leather jacket and skinny jeans. Her hair is loose and frames her tiny face. I like it when she doesn't use gel. I want to bury my face in her Afro and breathe her in. She hugs me and holds me and it's so nice just to lean my head against her shoulder and to let go. I take her hand, she walks me into the kitchen and I don't count. Ola's mopped everywhere and I wonder why he's cleaning when we haven't eaten yet. Dia sits me down at the table and pulls a bottle of brandy out of her bag. Dia always knows what to do.

'So, babe, how ya doing?'

'I'm fine, fine. There's so much to think about I can't think about anything, if you know what I mean.'

'I know, I know, take your time you don't have to think at all just now. Where's that girl?'

'Oh, she's at work, I have to go and pick her up in thirty-eight minutes. I can't drink.'

'You'll drink and I'll pick up, and I'll leave in forty-five minutes if that's okay with you.'

I want to touch Dia. I want to touch her and kiss her and be with her. But I can't. Ola's sitting at the table with us and I have to think about him. And our dead dad. I want to think about Dia but if I do I'll have to think about her leaving me. Though she can't right now because my dad's died. He nearly caught us the last time he was here. I told her we couldn't but she didn't listen and he nearly caught us and I didn't speak to her for weeks. Not until he'd gone home. And she told me I should grow up and be myself. We fought and then we loved and everything was okay again. She has her hand on my thigh and it's tingling and I want to kiss her, badly, but she's talking to Ola and she's so sweet. She squeezes my leg before she gets up and leaves to pick up Kutes.

16

Once they're back we eat and sit around the table chatting and drinking. I'm a bit worried that we're doing things wrong, not Nigerian enough, but I ask Ola and he says it's fine. And it doesn't make sense that I think we're not doing things right because dad wasn't Nigerian. He was bloody Mancunian. From Ardwick. As white, working class as they come. And I haven't thought about him like that before because he's always lived in Nigeria. But I suppose he became an honorary Nigerian at some point. He had kids there. He only married Nigerian women. My mum, Ola's mum. Dia is rubbing my arm and I realise I've been staring at the salt pot.

We chat about Dad and the nice things he said and did and the stories he loved to tell.

'Remember when he took us to Blackpool, Kutes? He hired that car and we thought it was gonna fall to bits. We were going to see the lights because your nan hadn't been for years or something. Yeah, you must remember. He was in one of his jokey moods. You loved it when he was like that. You could get anything out of him. I'm sure you got roller skates that trip.'

We don't talk about his last visit and the way he was with Mum and the fact that he was so rude and demanding and telling me someone had put juju on him. Or about the fact that I said I never wanted to see him again. The more I drink, the less real it seems that he's dead.

We all go quiet. Kutes gets hold of the brandy and starts to fill our glasses again, pouring the largest amount in her own, thinking I won't notice. As usual Dia jumps in before I can say anything.

'What about the stories he told you, as though you were a little girl not a forty year old woman.'

'Oh, god, yeah. They were like Anansi stories with a Manchester twist. He was hilarious when he was ready.'

Kutes rolls her eyes. She makes a point of scraping back her chair.

'I'm going up now. 'Night.' And she's gone, although from the music that's thumping through the ceiling she hasn't gone to bed. Ola follows. I fill the dishwasher and start to wash the pans. Dia is kissing my neck and running her hands down my back and I'm tempted to leave the kitchen, to let it wait, but I can't. When I've finished we go into the living room. Dia settles into one corner of the sofa, I lie against her and wrap us in my cream blanket. We don't put any music on.

'So, hon, have you talked to your mum?'

'Oh my god, no. No, I haven't. Damn!'

'It's okay, it's okay. You can ring her tomorrow, can't you? It'll be fine.

Come here.'

'What am I going to do, Dee? I don't know what to do about anything and I feel so crap and so useless and I hate it. All day I've been counting.' Dia strokes my hair and plants kisses around my face while she opens the buttons on my blouse. We try not to do this when Kutes is in the house but tonight I need her. Twisting round, I fold my fingers into her hair and pull her face towards me, kissing her roughly. I need to feel something. Dia knows. She pushes me back and bites my right nipple hard. The pain is good. She follows this with light kisses and teasing licks before biting again. I need her. Instead she pulls back. Begins to undo her shirt. She isn't wearing a bra. Her dark nipples are hard on her small breasts. She's teasing me. I follow her fingers down her flat stomach until she reaches her jeans. There's no zip, just buttons and she's popping them open, taking her time. I push my baggy jeans over my hips, wriggling from under her, my eyes not leaving her hands. Her skin mesmerises me. Smells of cocoa butter mixed with musky perfume surround us. When she stands to take off her jeans I have to stand with her, press myself against her before biting her on the shoulder. Pushing her back on to the sofa, I kiss every part of her until I can feel her vibrating. She pushes me roughly away so that I can watch her. She's so beautiful and I don't realise I'm crying until she pulls me on top of her and wraps her arms around me.

Kutes

Oi carls ya there
    yeah yeah how comes ya so late
    dunno had to nyam me food an that
    have they got owt new in today
    nah same old shit i swear i hate it in that place why can't i just slob
around like you
    ooooooh moody wots up babes
    nothin
    come on honey tell ya anty carly all about it
    me mums goin sick
    why wots up with her wot have ya done now hahahaha
    nah it's me grandad he's snuffed it innit
    no way kutes why dint ya say when ya come online nah thats bad man
wheres he live
    dunt live anywhere now does he hahahahahahahahahaha
    nah kutes dont be like that did he live with yer nan
    nah hes in nigeria innit ya no me mums brothers here and that well he
was cryin today so i just belled me mum an told her to get her arse home
i aint dealin with that shit
    yeah but hes a bit cute still innit i'd go there
    nah your sick ewwwwwwwwww thats like incest or summat
    hahahahahahahahahahahahaha dont be daft he aint my brotha
    talkin bout fit guys i swear these guys were like shoutin at me an
everythin when i was walkin up to work the driver was well fit
    so did ya get his number or wot
    nah don't be daft im wiv emre innit
    oh yeah I keep forgettin anyways whats yer mum gonna do now
    nowt it aint her probs is it but least olas gotta go home now thank fuck
then were movin to me nans house innit
    oh yeah i forgot wens that happnin
    dunno now cos shes goin a bit loopy anyways im gonna go ive got a
headache see ya tomorrow yeah
    yeah tomorrow give me a bell if ya wanna talk alrite

Ade

When we could view the port in Liverpool I was relieved at the thought of putting my feet on the earth again. The breeze was strong and cold and I shivered inside my woollen coat. James came to stand on the deck with me and slipped his hand into mine for just a moment.

'I'm sorry.'

'No Ade, I'm sorry. I'm really, really sorry.'

Tears slip out easily and James holds my hand tighter until I feel the bones squeezing against each other. A passenger beside James speaks,

'Yes. It's like that when you see the motherland. Tears. What a lucky girl you are. So many of your people would love to be where you are right now.'

James moves his body slightly to shield me from him. He holds me close to his side and though he doesn't say it, I know he loves me.

We took the overhead railway from Canada Docks. I remember the name because I thought we had reached the wrong continent when I saw it.

Watching the countryside flash past, pow-pow-pow! I was in another world. My curiosity squeezed itself through the sadness that had attached itself to me when I lost our baby. I believed each farm to be in a compound and was amazed at the size. Bigger even than my own family's.

'See the compounds, James.'

'They're farms.'

'And look at those animals!'

'Cows.'

'Eh-heh! They are so fat-o.'

James laughed at me and explained about fields and acres and such like. It was as though we had not left the bush as we sat close together whispering. Even Mrs Okorro joined in, asking questions of him.

We rushed through the countryside, the sun began to curtsey in a sky wrapped in purple clouds and it was dark by the time we arrived in Manchester. I pulled my case from the rack and stood with everyone else, eager to begin my new life. We stood on the platform and Mrs Okorro pushed a piece of paper with her address into my hand. The last time I saw her she was being lifted from the ground and swung around by a large man. We continued to write until she returned to Nigeria with three children and her freshly educated husband.

The walk through the streets to Manley Road had me gripping on to his arm. I was tripping to keep up with him. I thought the area dirty and broken down. James took giant strides, pointing out buildings and rubble that used to be buildings. He explained to me all about the bombing, but of course this meant nothing to a seventeen year old Nigerian girl who had no idea what a world war looked like.

We stopped in front of this house. It was balanced on top of itself. I thought, surely this house must fall down. My mouth was drier than the Harmattan. I knew from maps at the school mission that this England was a tiny country. I believed that they had built their houses up because they did not have enough room.

The house had windows, but there was nothing behind them, only blackness. Except for high up at the top where I could see a flicker of pale yellow. James nudged me to move me forward. The door was made of bad wood, frayed at the bottom like an old wrapper. Before James could pull at the piece of metal at the side of the door, it opened. A strange odour made me hold my nose. I did not think I could stay in this house. Its smells invaded me. James took a deep breath and smiled. He spoke to the woman at the door in a way that was too familiar. I recall the conversation exactly:

'Ooh! What a homecoming Mrs K. I haven't tasted cabbage and ribs for more than five years.'

'Oh, aye, and who says you'll be tasting them today?'

Mrs K is looking at me. Her dark brown eyes remind me of my own mama's and I catch my breath with the missing of her.

I bobbed my knee and lowered my head. James's fingers held me up and I realised that this is not the way to greet an elder in Manchester. Instead I smiled with my teeth and said,

'How does your house stay up? It is so tall.'

She turned around and walked down the hallway without answering me. James squeezed my arm and guided me in front of him and I kept my eyes on the black and white floor that had dirty footprints leading to the mirror at the foot of the stairs, the same one that still sits there. It is good for checking hair or hat as a person leaves the house. Its wooden frame fits the house well, but back then, all I could see was my own face, eyes wide open, looking like I had seen the water spirit.

We go up the dark stairs. Right up to the top. Sha! I think I will be sure to die when the house crashes down. I take each step slowly. Only at mission school have I taken steps before. These are wooden stairs, with patterned carpet and dark metal rods. I hold tightly to the smooth wooden rail and the wall. James runs up with my case in his hands. It's as though I'm climbing to the top of a rubber tree without a rope.

When we reach the first platform I let go of my breath. I do not dare to look behind me. But James carries on down the passageway. I begin to cry. I'm sure James is leading me to my death. The smell that met us at the door has lessened and is replaced with the smell of dust at the end of dry season when the first rains come.

Another corner. More stairs. Pale light is coming from an open doorway. The carpet that had run up the centre of the first flight and on along the hallway stops. I look just one step ahead with each footfall. I arrive on the small platform at the top and James pushes the room door open further. He points to the bed. The dresser. The window.

'This is all right, Ade. Look.'

Tears are building up and coming from deep inside of me and I can feel my mouth beginning to stretch. This is what I left my home for. James stands and looks at me. His arms are hanging by his side.

'Come on Ade, it's not that bad. Look you can see right across to the park. Well, nearly.'

'I want to go home. I cannot live here. What have I done?'

The metal bed dips down in the middle like a muddy riverbank. The carpet in the centre of the room is like dried grass in the middle of a drought. My toes are squeezed in my stiff leather boots. My coat is damp. James strides to the big window in the corner of the room. He throws it open, letting in rain.

You can smell the coldness coming from the window and from the blankets on the bed and from the rug on the floor. Even the paper on the walls, where James stands staring out, is hanging in shreds and the large pink flowers look as though they are wilting.

Elizabeth

When I wake up I'm in bed and I'm alone. Kutes is banging around in the kitchen. I think about Dia. I push my face into the pillow and can smell her hair oil, lemon and bergamot. Running my hands down my body I'm tempted to relive our time. I'm deciding which fantasy to go with, but other things are pushing into my mind and then I remember. My dad's dead. My skin starts itching on the inside.

Pushing back the covers and pulling on my kimono, I go downstairs and into the kitchen and am just in time to see the back of Kutes's head as she runs out of the door. I go back upstairs and shower. Just a bit of cleaning before I make a cup of tea. Damn, the bleach smells good. There are crumbs everywhere and I can see a scrape mark on the floor. I knew Kutes had marked it. While I'm mopping I notice some scuffmarks under the cupboards, on the boards that go across, and the mop won't bring them off. Ola comes downstairs.

'Sistah! Please stop. Let me, now. It's okay. Stop now.'

'I've nearly done. Put the kettle on.'

I let him take the cloth and the bowl away from me and lead me to the table.

'Has anyone phoned you? Did Tosan ring?'

'No, sistah, don't worry. I will speak to uncle later.'

'We have to go to the funeral. Do you know when it'll be? How soon?'

'It will be long, long before the funeral. There is too much to do and arrangements to make. I will go home to help my mama.'

'What do you mean you'll go home? When? What about me? I have to come too. I have to make arrangements.'

'No, sistah, I will go first, then you will come. It will be fine.'

How can it all be fine? My dad's dead and I have to go and bury him and tell my mum and go to Nigeria and I don't want to do any of it. Ola's talking to me but I can't stop, sixty, forty eight. He's shaking my hand.

'Sistah, please stop now? Will I call your friend to come? I have to go to school and make arrangements.'

'It's not school, it's uni or college. I've told you we don't say that here. School is for kids. You're an adult. You're doing a degree. And no, I'm fine, I'm all right. You go. I've got things to do.'

I'm fully aware that I have to go and see my mum. I shower again and clean the bathroom. I'm not sure how I'm going to tell her. I could grasp her hand and look her in the eyes, my own looking sad and defeated, ' I have something to tell you, I'm sorry.' That way I can drag it out and the tension will build. But that would make it about her and he's my dad. Was my dad, so it should probably be more about me. Maybe I should throw myself in her arms and weep, but then I am forty-four so that would be a bit weird. How the hell am I supposed to do it? But it might not even be bad news to her. She could have been waiting for thirty years for this and do cartwheels round the kitchen. What if she does that? It's my dad. She can't. That would be incredibly insensitive to my feelings.

It's twelve before I leave. I'm walking, which seemed like a good idea until my fingers start to tingle with the cold. I'm half way there so it doesn't make sense to go back for the car. And it's only a twenty minute walk. I can smell the frost even though it's not arrived yet. I'm not sure saris are warm enough for this weather. But it's nice to see the bright colours with gold threads sticking out beneath dark wool coats. Still, I think jeans would be better in October. I don't want to catch Sakhina's eye, I don't want to talk. Not that there's anything wrong with her but I'm not in the mood. I'm sure she can't be warm enough. Mind you, that Mrs Phiri from number 10 always wears African clothes and I know they're not made for winter. I hate the sound of those bloody street cleaners. I'm cold.

Kutes

I dont know any other dead people well I dont know me grandad either do I really think I only ever saw him twice well probs more than that cos like me mum said he used to buy me stuff an I do remember us going out and that but later he was a bit freaky it aint like anyone wanted him here an he was poncin round the house like he owned it but I know he dint cos me nan showed me the deeds like a thousand times an told me the friggin story bout how she bought it with her own money blah blah blah wonder what its like to be dead an not to feel anythin or see anythin or think that would be the worst thing not bein able to think do ghosts think or do they just do things wonder what its like not to think when I told emre he was like all superstish an sayin bout the evil eye an shit an I was like yeah woteva an he said I shunt be thinkin bout dead peeps like that but it was me grandad so itd be weird if I dint think bout him even if I dint know him proper sometimes emres not right

Ade

I did not sleep well. My hip is aching. I will not have the operation though. Not at my age. Perhaps I should have telephoned Elizabeth yesterday. I am sure the boy, Ola, will have informed her what has happened. Ah, well, she will come. I must cook some food. First, I will have a cup of tea to warm me through. I miss my old kettle. It was the original one that belonged to Mrs Kingsley. Back in those days everything was made to last. Unlike now. This electric kettle that Elizabeth insists I use does not make a proper cup of tea. The water does not boil, as it should. And it is made from plastic. I am sure I can taste it when I drink. I remember my first cup of real English tea. The day we arrived.

Mrs Kingsley is at the door of my room and I do not know how long she has been there. I stand, my hands on my belly holding in the loss of everything. She has a china cup in her hand and speaks to me kindly. I remember her words:

'Hey, lass, there's no need for all that now, is there?'

I do not know what a lass is, but I know she means me. James closes the windows and walks towards the door, patting me on the shoulder as he passes. She hands me the cup. It is very small and delicate, not like the large tin mug I use at home, it is hot and I needed to drink it quickly to get the heat inside me. Mrs Kingsley speaks very slowly to me and moves her mouth in a funny way:

'You'll be all right after that cuppa. Get it down you.'

'Thank you. I am sorry.'

'It's understandable lass. You come downstairs once you've settled. We're having a meeting.'

She points downstairs and makes gestures that somehow suggest I should follow her. I know the word 'meeting'.

Rubbing me on the back, she smiles and leaves the room. The tears threaten to start again. Mama's voice comes clear inside my head. As though she is standing behind me.

'Consequences, Adeola. There are consequences for every action. Is it not so? Why then are you crying?'

I drink my tea, which is bitter and does not have much milk. It burns my mouth in a different way to pepper soup, but it is warm and holding the thin cup helps my fingers to feel again. I do not want to leave it in the bedroom to encourage insects so when I have finished I carry it down those terrible stairs. At any moment I expect to crash down to the ground with this building all around me. I am walking into darkness with my own body blocking the light from the room I have just left. With my free hand I feel my way along the corridor and the rough paper on the walls scrapes at my skin.

I reach the main staircase and I can see again. I go down as quickly as I possibly can and stand in the hallway with its black and white floor. I can hear voices. There is a cold breeze coming from the front door. My bones rub against each other. The delicate teacup begins to feel very heavy in my hand. I hold it with palms that are sweating as though I was in the midday sun. I fear I will drop it on the hard floor and it will smash into a hundred pieces.

Hei, was I really so young and frightened at one time? It is difficult to believe that now. Especially when I look at my own granddaughter and see that she is fearless. But wait, was not I myself also fearless? I left my home. I travelled across the world. I made decisions about my own life.

I stood listening to the voices in one of the rooms. I am sure I would still be standing there now if the front door had not pushed open. As my eyes adjusted I thought it was uncle. The shape of his head with untidy hair not cropped close enough. The shape of his shoulders. I felt so sure I opened my mouth and almost shouted 'uncle' but as he moved closer I realised I was mistaken. This man was much younger and the heavy coat he wore caused his size to appear much larger, and, in fact, his head was covered in a flat hat. I have never forgotten the first words he spoke to me:

'How now, sistah, how are you today?'

'You are welcome.' I answered without thinking, I was so happy to hear his voice. It was only then I realised that since leaving the boat in Liverpool I had not heard my own accent.

He walked to the far end of the hallway. I followed him so quickly I stood on the back of his shoe and he almost left it behind. He limped into the room and I heard him say,

'Hey, this one has just come from the boat, sha! I shall marry her today before she unlearns all that her mother taught her.'

Everybody was laughing at me. I did not dare to lift my head.

James shouted at me to close the door. I looked towards his voice and he had a frown on his face. Quickly closing it I stood with my back leaning on it and looked around the room. There were about ten people sitting around a large table. I counted seven men as well as James and one other old white man and Mrs Kingsley. The room was very warm and I could smell a fire burning. Of course, James had told me of this so I was not alarmed.

I looked around, worried in case I did the wrong thing. Behind the table on the back wall was a large wooden cabinet. It was piled high with books and papers, so I moved my eyes to the wall opposite me where there was an iron cabinet which held a steaming pot, larger than any I had seen before, even Mama's soup pot was not that big, and there was fire underneath it. I knew it was the cooker. James promised me that I would have a house with a gas cooker when we got to England and I was fascinated to see one. I did not know I had not moved until James came and took the cup from me and gripped my shoulder and showed me a chair.

It was the big-armed, big-backed, leather chair and I sat myself down in it. I almost disappeared I am sure. It was very hard and though I believed it would be cold it was hot to touch because it was placed next to the fire. I kept that chair for thirty-five years until Elizabeth decided that I should be modernised. Now I have this flimsy replica, sha!

From behind the wing on the chair I could see everybody at the table and once the meeting began I could look at them easily. They were all dressed the same, except of course Mrs Kingsley. The men, they had on shirts and ties and woollen sweaters. Very dark colours and not at all comfortable looking. Mrs Kingsley had on a plain coloured dress. I do not remember the colour but probably it was grey or brown because those are the only colours I ever saw her wearing . Her cardigan was pushed up her arms so I could see her wrists, which were very pale. She had one thin gold bracelet on her right wrist and she constantly moved it up her arm so that she could rest her hand on the book she was writing in. I wondered why she would be writing during a meeting.

The old man banged his hand on the table and two of the men who had been talking loudly to each other stopped. He said something I could not catch and everyone looked at him. James began to talk about my village and I did not recognise any of it. He said its men were weak and unschooled, but willing. Weak and unschooled? What a thing to say. And how wrong he was. I leaned back in the chair and listened instead to the scratch of the pen going across the paper, as Mrs Kingsley wrote and wrote. Every now and then there was a rustle like dried leaves as she turned the page. The fire on my right side had burned low and I could hear it crackling and hissing. The pan further along was popping.

Elizabeth

I open the front door. The black and white tiles scream at me. I had a game when I was young that I could only step on the black tiles. It was important not to stand on the cracks. 'Cos if you stand on a line, you'll marry a swine and beetles will come to your wedding'. I feel sick.

Once, I'd walked through the hallway not bothering where I put my feet. Then that man. He'd been coming down the stairs, not one of Mum's tenants. He was definitely a visitor because Mum only rented to African students and their families and he wasn't African or my dad. I'd been running to get to the ice cream van and I ran straight into him as he turned the corner of the stairs. He put his hand under my chin and smiled at me. There was a hair sticking out of his nose. I just wanted to go. I went to dash out of the door but he wouldn't let me go. He stroked me. He turned me round and stroked me again, running his hand right down my back and across my bottom. He smelt of cigarettes. He was laughing. Then mum was there, hitting him with the Ewbank. He ran out, mum cussing him from the front door. The tenants came down as she was cussing and two of the students ran out into the street but he was gone. After that I made sure I only walked on the black tiles.

There are two masks on the wall at the bottom of the stairs, and an old mirror in between. I brought the masks back from Nigeria when I went in 1996. They're black and slim and delicate. When I was coming home with them the soldiers wanted to search my suitcase. It was military rule then and the airport was full of men with guns. I refused but Aunty Funmi's daughter, who had taken me to the airport, made me stand back and she opened my case. When they found the masks they decided I needed a certificate to take them out of the country. I told them to keep them. I knew they wanted money. She took the soldiers to one side and talked and in the end they allowed them through and I brought them home.

The mirror looks rusty in patches. The other long wall is busy with flocked wallpaper that's rubbed smooth in places. It'll be strange to call this house home again. Twenty-two years I've been away from here. It feels right. Mum's getting older. She doesn't go upstairs anymore. The house would have fallen to pieces if I hadn't had the work done. It's happening all around here. Big, old, beautiful houses falling apart. They sit there in their overgrown gardens with bits falling off them. At the back of the hallway the glass in the door to the bathroom is reflecting the light from the small window inside.

'Elizabeth! What you dey do? You come now. Right now.'

The light goes on and Mum's standing at her door with her hands on her hips. I walk straight up to her and she gets hold of me tight. I'm crying. She feels so small now. I can't remember the last time I hugged her. As usual she smells of tiger balm. Her short hair is neat and soft and gently curled. She must have been to the hairdresser's. She still starches her clothes. I can feel the stiffness in the material. I got her a lovely housedress thing but she insists on her African prints. I need a tissue.

Mum leads me to the table and although it's only 12.15, there's a bowl of egusi soup and a smooth round of eba.

'So daughter, talk to me.'

'Err, Dad, he, I don't know, Ola got a phone call. Yesterday afternoon.'

'Sis Funmi telephoned me, also. I know what has happened.'

'I don't understand, he was just ill. Tosan didn't ring back. I don't know what to do. I have to go there. Ola's going soon, but I have to go.'

'Don't worry, daughter. We will all go. It will be fine.'

'I'm waiting for more information. Ola will tell me what to do. I want to know when the funeral will be, I have to go to it.'

'Of course we have to go. It will be well, you will see.'

I'm not convinced. I don't stay long.

31

Kutes

dont even know why I bothered goin round to see her when I couldve got a lift home from college cos emre said hed pick me up yeah an now ive gotta walk home and its friggin freezin

it aint fair that I have to feel guilty an shit when ive got me a levels but I dint think me mum would go round the way shes goin on with herself an someone had to go an see me nan an emre was like well I can come with yer innit an Im like derrrr! no yer cant and then he starts goin on bout I shunt be bothered what anyone thinks an its okay for us to be together blah blah so Im like yeah cos me nan would love it if I turns up with someone an I aint told her bout you already I dint say someone old enough to be me dad but he probly knew I meant that an now hes gonna sulk innit

today was real good as well so I dint really need no shit from him or anyone really cos we finished our project and me an carls are gonna present it next week and we no were gonna win cos aint no one else put together a presentation like ours cos weve been spyin an if we win we get to take it to the town hall and present it there cos we have a right to influence policy teach says cos were that ones that get affected an anyways human rights is a good thing to no about even if we don't win cos weve all got rights innit though you wunt think so if you was me I swear

an then when I gets to me nans she dint even know it was me callin me daughter an shit an I was like bein really nice to her cos it was her husband that died innit an then shes sayin she cant hear me needs a hearin aid I reckon its not like im speakin French is it or like when Ola came an he was talkin like his mouth wunt move an I was supposed to understand that

an me nans been here forever so it aint like cho they all need to get a friggin grip innit an then shes goin on like were all goin to nigeria as if

nobody told him to live there so why should we have to go anyways I aint goin no friggin way its not like its on the holiday show is it like jamaica or sum cool island nope I aint goin thanks for askin but I aint effin goin when ive got exams an shit nope it aint happnin

Ade

When my daughter arrives at lunchtime I watch her for a while. She looks around my hallway and her eyes are wild. There is distaste written in the frown on her forehead and she is planning the changes she will make when she returns. We will discuss this.

'Elizabeth, what are you doing? Come in and close the door. It is cold.'

It has been long since she has thrown her arms around me and cried. Not since she was very young. We come into the kitchen and I sit her at the table. Egusi soup warms her.

'Do not cry child, all will be well.'

'But Papa has died, I don't know what to do.'

'Can I not tell you?'

Elizabeth forgets that I am African. She thinks that because the boy, Oladayo, speaks native he is more authentic than myself. And what of my granddaughter? What kind of language does she speak? It will be good to take her home. It is only right that we all pay our respects. What would people think if we did not?

On my first night here, James was shaking me awake. I did not know where I was. I had been at home. In Papa's compound. Cooking with Mama and my sister, Funmi. The sun was hot on my cheek. It took me a while to remember I was in England.

Only four people were left in the room, Mrs Kingsley, James, the man Olu, who wanted to marry me, and the old man. My leg, arm and right side of my face were very hot and I yawned loudly, forgetting myself.

'Come on Ade, we're eating.'

Olu laughed at me and I decided I did not like him. I made the mistake to go and sit next to Mrs Kingsley, which meant that I had to sit opposite this Olu. He kept trying to catch my eye and wink at me. And he had only just met me. He had not even asked of my father. I put a big frown on my face and stared into my bowl. Broth, James said it was called. Rations, Mrs Kingsley added. I thought it was water, with very little salt and no pepper and green leaves floating in it. I did not know at that time what rations were, but I knew I did not want to eat them again. It was only my rumbling belly that caused me to spoon it into my mouth.

The old man had not spoken to me. He fixed his eyes on me. His grey whiskers hid most of his expression.

'Ah, a village girl. What of your family?'

He spoke to me but I did not say anything because as far as I could tell he had not asked me a question and I did not like him.

'She's a bit shy. There are two girls. It's strange really, only girls. Her dad works for the foreign office, you know, trying to get others in line. Anyway, she's here to study and then we'll go back. Probably take over the compound at some point. You know, with her being the eldest.'

'So what's the village like then? Are they working towards an uprising? Do they understand what we're doing for them?'

I glared at James while he started telling that old man about the meetings my own Papa held.

'They're trying. You know, it's a bit difficult. A bit cut off. No sense of urgency. But that happens when you give them good jobs. The ones who could make a difference are too comfortable.'

I was not happy. The old man nodded and eh-heh'd, without taking his eyes from my face. My throat had already been struggling to swallow this broth and now it did not want to open again. Olu interrupted James, and said good things about our country. Truthful things. That old man, Charles, nodded his head and agreed that yes we were in some ways quite clever, and then he laughed. I knew by the way that Olu tightened his mouth and pulled together his eyebrows that he felt the same burn in his belly that I did. I could not say that they were laughing at us because I did not understand what Charles meant, but I disliked him even more.

Olu put down his spoon, thanked Mrs Kingsley graciously and fitted his heavy overcoat on to his shoulders. I panicked because suddenly I did not want to be left alone with these strangers. I jumped up so quickly my chair almost fell over and broth splashed over the side of the bowl as I knocked the handle of my spoon. I followed him out of the door and the hallway was dark and cold after the heat of the kitchen and I felt my skin tighten. Olu strode ahead of me to the door and pulled it open.

'It would seem you are keeping bad company, Ade.'

'No, not James, he did not mean anything. He is friends with my Papa.'

'Really, Ade? Are you sure about that?'

Of course I was sure. James loved me. But still I felt as though part of me was leaving with Olu and I did not want him to go. I wanted to go home.

The door opened behind us and Olu turned and went down the path out into the street. The rain had stopped and it was a pale dark. It was strange to me how the dark failed to arrive. At home you can blink your eye and it will go from day to night but here in Manchester it took me a while to understand that night never came because of streetlights.

The old man, Charles, walks towards the door. Even though I do not turn I can hear his breathing, which comes out like it is forced and makes his chest rattle. As he passes me his hand touches my backside. I believe it is accidental until it happens again and I realise he is patting me as though I am an animal. On my backside. I want to pull his grey whiskers from his face and spit in his eye, but instead I turn and run back to the kitchen.

When we made that treacherous climb to my room I told James exactly what I thought about him and his friends, I slapped his face and I cried and he tried to make me laugh. But you see, the whole day had been so very long and tiring I could not arrange myself. I had left my home without saying goodbye to my mama, I had lost a baby that was my whole reason for leaving and now this man who I thought I loved was laughing at me. He put his arm around my shoulder.

'Don't worry, Ade. Everything will be fine.'

'No, it will not. You said bad things about my papa.'

'But Ade I only said what Charles wanted to hear. It was nothing. It meant nothing. You don't understand how these things work.'

I doubted this entirely, but there was little I could do at that moment. I placed my photograph of Mama and Papa on the table and covered the sagging bed with my favourite wrapper. When James was ready to leave I was not sorry. I needed time to think. So that was my first day in my new home. I had been laughed at, proposed to, disturbed and attended one meeting, although I slept throughout.

Despite my nervousness about how the building would remain standing, I fell into that metal bed gratefully. It was cold and damp and the smell was not pleasant, but I wrapped myself in my own cloth and looked through the window. I could see the moon and I wondered how it could be so small.

35

Elizabeth

Two weeks and four days since 'the phonecall' and Ola's gone home. Just like that, he goes and it's almost as though he's never been here and dad hasn't died and everything's normal. But really, it's so strange. We're all waiting. Me, Mum, Kutes. But we're not waiting together, it's like we're in some kind of weird circle dance. Kutes is completely indifferent, Mum's off in some other place that requires a lot of muttering and now really isn't the time for her to be losing her marbles. So, even when we come together, we're still on our own. Waiting. And, on top of everything, I have to begin packing.

We've been in this house for twelve years and I'm not sure about leaving. We've been happy here. It's like we moved in and good things came my way, like my job and Dia. But in the past six months it's all gone to shit like it was building up to dead dad day. Kutes grew up really quickly, I'd been waiting since she started puberty for this monster to come out but it never did. She was a bit moody, but just the same as always. Smiley, sweet and cuddly. Then she turned seventeen and damn it must have all been lurking under that niceness. Dia said I'm making it up, that nothing changed except me, but that's not true. My little girl left me and was replaced by a person who I don't know. Someone who doesn't listen or care about anything.

I decided to move back to Mum's in June. She's getting older and Kutes is getting older and it just makes sense. Not that I don't like my house, but I can't exactly kick Kutes out or bring Mum here. My house is small and we need our own space. It was Dad's. He bought it when he came home one time and said I should rent it out for him. I couldn't be bothered. I had my job, Kutes was in school, we had our own cute little flat on Stretford Road and I didn't see why I should do it for him. I didn't owe him anything. I can't remember the conversation but I'm sure I would have been a bit off with him. I was like that back then. I don't know why. Maybe it was postnatal depression. But Kutes was five so I hardly think so. Before he went back to Nigeria he gave me the keys and told me I should live there because it was bigger and had a garden. Mum helped me to move. I think it was probably her decision.

Like I told Dia, I'm not really moving back home. It's like separate flats. It is Mum's house technically but it's big enough so that we all have our own rooms. My cream rug will stay cream. Mum must be lonely. It took some convincing but finally Dia gets it because since 'the phonecall' even she can see that Mum is kind of looking older and a bit frail and the house is so bloody big.

All the cardboard boxes are flat and labelled in the shed. I've only got to make them up and begin to pack.

Typical. The minute I get up to do something the phone starts ringing. I know it's Ola.

'Hello, sistah. Is it you? Are you well?'

'Ola, are you okay?'

'Sistah, everyone is fine. We are making the arrangements now. There is a family meeting this afternoon. Do you have anything for me to say?'

'Like what? I don't know.'

'Well, we will arrange when the funeral is to take place. You are the eldest child so you can say what you think.'

'Erm, I don't know. It's been two weeks and four days already. I have to move house. How long does it usually take? Where's dad's body?'

'He is in the morgue. Not to worry. Sometimes it will take long. It is the money.'

'Right, okay. I'll speak to my mum later and see what she thinks.'

Bloody family meeting. How can they have a family meeting? I'm family. I won't be there. My dad wasn't even Nigerian. He was British for god's sake. He was brought up in bloody Ardwick. How can someone who was brought up in bloody Ardwick have people holding meetings to decide how he's buried? It's bloody ridiculous. But I suppose it isn't. He lived there for about forty years, probably more because he was there way before I was born. That mean's he lived there longer than mum did. Does that make him Nigerian? Does it make mum British? Or is it all about where you're born. Or is it your passport?

Oh, god, my head hurts. I'll have to go to London to get a visa. I'd forgotten about that. I wonder if Dad had a Nigerian passport. He must have. He couldn't just live there without something. I never thought about that before. God, he was more Nigerian than my mum. Which is ridiculous.

List:

1.Download visa applications

2.Complete visa applications with black ink

3.Make an appointment at the embassy

4.Book train tickets

5.Book a hotel near to the embassy

6.Send sick note to work
7.Pack up house
8.Clean house
9.Clean new house
10.Move to new house
11.Have a break down!

I just want to go and bury my dad. Why the hell do I have to go through all of this visa business? And for Kutes as well. And I don't know if my mum is going. I don't think she needs to. It's not as though they were married-married. I mean conventionally married. Oh, of course they were. They got married here in the registry office. Of course they were married. But I don't know if that counts in Nigeria. I'll ring her, I'll check.

'Hello'

'How now, daughter, how are you?'

'Hi, Mum, I'm fine. I was just going to ring you, and then I didn't because I didn't want to disturb you. I don't know wh...'

'Do not worry, it will be well, it will be fine. Are you coming?'

'Yes, yes. I'll come now. I'm coming now.'

Kutes

No way are we movin in 2 weeks I cant wait itll be so cool like havin me own flat and carls can come an stay an its like I don't have to ask permission an the house is well nice now except for that ugly stuff in the hallway but I might paint it white an we could get some carpet down an it'd look like a proper house

dunno why shes only given me 6 boxes like I can get me whole life into that an it aint even like theyre big ones but I bet she worked out the square meter of me room and divided it by the number of things in it or summat mental like that

no way have I still got that history book me an carls proper graffitied over it an I was like in love with nuff guys in me last year haha but callums got the most love hearts I need to keep that innit but I better hide it cos emre gets well jel sayin stuff bout the lads at college shit is that me baby book I forgot she gave me that ewww I was a well ugly baby why do people take pictures when their sprogs just dropped out an theyre all screwed up just me an a hand holdin me in the pic

I can tell thats me mums hand cos its light skin and its still the same shape now but more red cos of all her friggin cleanin an that ones me nans cos it looks like treacle toffee an its dead little her hands are tiny I wish mine were like hers but theyre not cept me nails theyre neat an round

jeez how many pictures of an ugly baby do ya need hang on whos hands that one it aint me grandad cos it aint white but its defo a man cos I can see his gross trousers puke green colour an it aint anyone who knows us cos I aint seen mum near a man shes only ever been with aunty dia even though she thinks I dont know bout that whatever

no way I bet its me dad I bet it is and she says she dint know him proper an he never saw me I swear down if it is nah that aint right

Ade

My children are returning home. I thought I would go crazy with all the movement upstairs. Bang, bang bang, every day from early morning until late afternoon with only respite for lunch. Modernising. What is this modernising? This house is as solid as the day I moved into it.

There was nothing the workers did not touch. I told them every day. Do not throw anything away without me seeing it first. I am sure they did not listen. Every article in this house holds its own story and some stories I did not want to disappear. Perhaps they have disturbed spirits who have been quietly sharing this space with me. But maybe that is a good thing. James will not find his way back easily.

This has been my home for sixty years and it is still my home. I did not believe it could be so when I first arrived. In my first few days here I curled into my wrapper, smelling of Mama and Funmi. I worried that I had made a mistake and that James did not love me. I felt as though I had eaten bad food, the pain in me was very physical. It passed, as these things do, but at that time it was as though I would never be well again. I could not allow myself to think about why I had come to this England or I would drown in my tears. One week passed but it felt like one month.

Mrs Kingsley had been very kind and had brought rations for me right up to my room. I had been so miserable I did not notice how hungry I was. When finally I decided that I had things I must do, I had a visitor. It was that cheeky man, Olu. I wanted to be quiet with him but I could not. When Mrs Kingsley came to knock on my door, he was standing right behind her and I am sure she must have asked him to wait downstairs. Before she could say anything his big voice was filling the room.

'Come on Ade, let us go for a walk. It is a lovely day.'

And he stepped straight into my room. Even Mrs Kingsley did not say anything to him. Ah, that Oluwaseun was always full of life.

Once she had left us, he started poking around with my belongings. I wanted to be cold towards him, but I was so very lonely.

'Where are you hiding it, Adeola?'

The man was cheeky-o. But I laughed.

'I know you have some dry meat.'

'And maybe some chin-chin? Perhaps I have a goat in there. Or Kola nut and palm wine.'

He was sure Mama had sent me with something he could eat. How was he to know my own mama did not know where I was? This Olu, he brought the hot African sunshine into my grey room. I had to open my box and show him that I was not hiding any home food from him.

I had left some wrappers in there because I did not feel to put them in the drawers of the dressing table in the cold room. I looked among them with great acting, for Olu was causing me to play. At the bottom of the box I felt something in wax paper. For one moment I thought that Funmi had placed some dry meat for me, but I could not smell anything. By instinct I did not mention what I had found and continued to play act for him. When he was satisfied I was not hiding anything I closed up my case and placed it in the corner by the wicker chair and the small dressing table. Putting on my coat, scarf, hat and gloves, I went and stood by the door. I was still anxious about the stairs but I had decided that the house would not be falling down any time soon.

We walked and talked, or I should say that Olu talked.

'Ade, things are going to change. It's happening. You wait and see. They are listening now. They must listen. We are going to rule ourselves.'

He was so full of ideas and he made it all sound so very easy. He talked about countries, which were simply names in my old geography book. I was young. I was excited. I did not understand how this cold country could help us. These white people were so miserable, I thought, that they seemed to need our help more. Olu explained to me about the war. About what had happened when Manchester was blitzed. But the most important thing was that now it was our time and we were going to do it. We were going to be free and rule ourselves and be a force in the world. Our Africa would be great. By the time we reached back to Manley Road we were laughing like children-o and I was forgetting some of my pain.

Elizabeth

Who's knocking on the frigging door like that when I've got so much to do? I'll ignore it. I'll go through to the hallway to get the buckets. I've got too much to do and it'll only be the Mormons or someone about the electric and I don't need to change my religion or the electric, or the gas, or my phone.

'Beth, Beth, it's me. I can see you. Come on, open the door.'

It's Dia.

'Oh my god, Beth. Are you okay? I'll make you a brew. Come on, hon.'

'There's nothing wrong. I just didn't hear the door.'

'No Beth, you've got buckets in your hands and you're crying. Come on now. It's all right, it's okay. Come on, let's get this door closed and go into the kitchen. That's better, come on now.'

'What are you doing here, Dia?'

'I was at a meeting up the road, finished early so I thought I'd check in on you.'

'I was writing a list and then I just kind of lost it.'

'Your dad's died. Don't be so hard on yourself.'

We had argued. A lot. And I didn't say sorry. Not that I was wrong. I know I wasn't wrong. He was being a right bastard. Oh, jeez, now I've thought it. I didn't mean to think it. But you can't help your thoughts, can you? It's not like I was sat here saying, ooh, I think I'll have bad thoughts about my dad. And it wasn't that bad. It was the truth. Does that count though? If it's true? Maybe I just don't think about him at all. It shouldn't be that difficult. I probably spent five years with him in total. Five years out of forty-four. That's nothing. I've spent more time sleeping. It's probably more than five years though, but I can't count when I was small and he was here because he was hiding. And anyway he didn't stay with us all the time. I don't even know when that was. The Biafran war. Of course it was. He came home when he found out it was going to happen. How do I know that? I was only about six at the time. So I couldn't know he was hiding. What the hell was he hiding from?

'My dad was hiding.'

'What, love? Hiding from what? Did Ola call you? Was something going on out there?'

'No, I mean, yes, Ola called. But I'm talking about when I was a kid. When it was the Biafran war.'

'I'm sure he wasn't, honey. Although he was a bit of a communist if I remember right, so maybe he was.'

'What do you mean, he was a communist? How do you know that and I don't?'

'Easy, I just listen to your mum's stories whereas you, lady, tune her out.'

I feel betrayed. Like I'm on the outside. So my mum, my girlfriend and probably my own bloody daughter know something about my dad that I don't. He was my dad. Oh, god, I sound like a teenager.

'There you go, that'll help.' Dia puts a cup of tea in front of me and it's not on a placemat and I want to shout at her because it'll mark the table, but I control myself and move it on to a coaster.

'I don't know if I can do it Dee. I don't think I can go to the funeral.'

'Okay. We can talk about that, can't we sweetie? When is it anyway?'

'If I knew when it was happening I'd be all right, wouldn't I? If I knew what I had to do I wouldn't be sitting here writing bloody lists. I'd be doing something.'

'Drink your tea, Beth, we'll sort it out. It'll be fine. Come on now, take some deep breaths.'

I need someone else to tell me what I should be doing. All I can do is cry, great big gulping, unattractive sobs. Dia puts a box of tissues in front of me and lets me get on with it. When I calm down she gives me a hug.

'No. I'm not going to Nigeria. Remember last time.'

'Okay. But Beth nothing happened last time. You went, you came back early – you were only gone a couple of days! And you've seen your dad plenty of times since then so...'

'What do you mean nothing happened. It made me ill, don't you remember?'

And I look at her hard because I can't believe what she's saying. I was ill. I went out to see my dad and his other family, Ola's family, and it should have been okay, but when I got back strange things kept happening and it was the red dust that did it. The red dust got everywhere and there were footprints and feathers and all sorts of things going on and it made me ill.

'Beth, you were a bit extreme when you came back for a while, but you stopped it and you were fine. You were stressed out before you went and pretty much the same when you came back. Remember when we were at school, I don't know, maybe the third year or something, you had little rituals that we all had to do. It's just how you were, how you are. There's nothing wrong with you. It doesn't make you ill, just a little different.'

Dia's looking at her watch. She has to go but she makes sure I leave with her, so I can't start cleaning, she says.

Kutes

Wot if me nans house is haunted that would be so cool cept it wud be all Africans innit cos thats all who lived there I dont remember any1 but me nan says she had tenants there woz always loadz of women in me nans kitchen wen me mum went to work she left me there an me nan wud play wiv me an then the other women that were there sometimes brought their kids or grankids or summat but I hated it cos then I had to share me biscuits wiv em dunno how old I was mustve been before I went to school innit else I wudnt have been there in the day time I did used to go in the holidays tho when we was at primary school cos I used to have me friends over an we played upstairs so there werent anyone livin there then cept that old woman who stunk but she dint bother us an we were allowed to run up an down the stairs an play hide an seek in all the rooms cept hers

so it was wen I was telling emre hes like so it is a big house you are movin to perhaps I may come and see it with you an im like nah dont think so cos me nans got ears like a friggin bat or summat an there aint no way I can sneak a bloke in cos shell know cos of your feet innit and then hes like whisperin in me ear and it tickles an is a bit wet I hate it when he does that he thinks its sexy or summat but I dont an I still aint givin him any an when I was tellin him bout me baby pics he was like why do you need a dad you have me now I will look after you an its like he dunt know how dam creepy that sounds cos hes like me boyfriend so why wud I wanna think of him like me dad ewww thats just plain gross

Ade

Still I did not want to be here, despite the time I had spent with that Olu. It was too strange. Everywhere I looked I saw white faces, and I felt like a foreigner. When I was at home I never once questioned who or what I was. I was simply Ade. My mama and papa were who they were and James was white, he was the foreigner. Of course, I did not think about that at the time. When he came to our compound for business I did not think about speaking to him to find out who he was. Until he came visiting.

I was thirteen when Papa started holding his late night meetings. I had seen the papers that were being handed out. Of course, we were not allowed to read them in school. But always they appeared in the back of someone's logarithms book. Why they thought we children would be interested I do not know. Unions, workers' rights, independence. The nuns soon put a stop to it and I forgot until Papa's meetings began.

The first time I listen it is by accident. It is Harmattan and I am so hot I cannot sleep. I pull my wrapper over my nightdress and tuck it under my arm. Feeling through the thick heat and darkness I push through the curtain into the passageway. There's a lamp outside that shows me the door is open and I walk towards it, hoping there will at least be a slight breeze. The sound of the night insects, hck, hck, hck, fill the darkness and moths hitting the lamp, add the high notes, ksss, ksss, ksss. A mosquito attaches itself to my arm and I quickly swat it away.

The air is no easier to breathe outside. The compound walls hold in the heat of the day. Trap it until it becomes thick like semolina. I stand in the doorway briefly before turning to go back to my bed. I hear the voices. I have to strain through the heat to make sense of what is being discussed. Papa makes his best laugh, the one he uses when he is with strangers. Uncle Tunde's voice bounces around too. The other's I do not recognise.

Somehow, I know it is about the leaflets and I am scared and excited at the same time. I want to creep to the corner to see who is speaking this kind of English. As I put my foot out of the door a hand touches my arm and I nearly scream. From the light of the lamp I see that it is James. Of course I do not know his name. He is simply one of the English drivers who sometimes comes to pick Papa up when he is needed somewhere urgently. My heart beats, pah-pah-pah! But his mouth is smiling so I know that he will not give me away.

I have never been so close to him before. I want to touch his hair that flops over his forehead. The lamp behind him makes it look like thick golden webs. It is so strange. I stop myself and pull my wrapper tighter around me, step back into the doorway. It is not proper that someone like James should see me in my nightclothes.

'I won't tell. This can be our secret, picken, isn't it?'

And I have to hold a laugh in because it sounds funny when white men try to speak in pidgin. I bid him goodnight and feel my way down the corridor to my room. Reaching my bed I shake Funmi awake.

'Sistah, I am in love.'

We whisper the night away.

It was much later when I realised the kind of meeting Papa was holding should not have included the Englishman who drove him. After Papa's first meeting that night he held many more. I learned when they were going to be by watching Mama. She was sad on meeting days. Sad and careful. Whether she was tying her wrapper or cooking in the outside hut.

She would tell me parables while I stirred the pot of soup, adding the chopped up yam at just the right time. Too soon and it softens to nothing, too late and it will not cook in time. Next to me Mama was preparing the starch so that it was round and smooth. She tested it by pinching and twisting a small piece from the mound. The parables were always the same. About an animal that did not know that it was well off until it did something stupid. I knew she was talking about Papa and I was both frightened and excited. I stirred my excitement into the soup until it smelled just right for serving. I spooned out my fear, leaning low over the pot with the pepper, making my eyes water. Mama's stories kneaded and patted the starch into yellow, fluorescent mounds. Those evenings I did my chores slowly. I waited for Mama to go to her room.

Elizabeth

It's really mild today. You wouldn't think it was November. I don't know what I'm going to say to Mum when I get there. It's like Dad dying has made us different people. And it doesn't help that I'm in a stinking mood now. Dia is so out of order sometimes. It's like she doesn't think before she opens her mouth. Things did happen when I went to Nigeria last time. I don't even know why I went. It was that group I was in, politics. I wanted to ask Dad why he thought it was acceptable to live in Africa, him being a white man. They said I was to go and educate him. Yeah, right. God, we were so up ourselves. But I also wanted to get away from Dia and Femi for a while. I was confused. Femi felt so familiar and I was starting to get comfortable with him. But then there was Dia and we were starting, I don't know, something. There was a change with us. She'd finished with her girlfriend and, well, it just felt right. It was the year before I had Kutes. If I hadn't gone I probably wouldn't have had her. Not that I regret it, no, I'm just thinking. It was all the weirdness. I don't know. Ola's mum. She did something.

Well, of course, logically, she didn't do anything. It's not like I believe in stuff like that. But it was strange. Maybe I should have told someone to expect me. But I didn't have to. He was my dad before he was anyone else's. I had the right to go and see him whenever I wanted. I booked a couple of weeks off work and told Mum I was going on holiday with my mates. Not that I had to tell her anything, I was old enough to do what I wanted. So I went. I got a visa, booked my flight and went. I was so scared when I got to the airport. I mean in Lagos. I didn't have a clue what I had to do. I hadn't been there since Mum took me when I was ten. It was all bustle and army. When they asked me why I was there, I got confused and said something stupid and they laughed at me. I thought they were going to stop me. Green uniforms and guns. That's how I remember it.

When I got through and was standing outside the terminal, men were coming up to me. Men in old dashiki shirts with wet patches under the arms. The sweat on their faces looked like it had been placed there, like it was waiting to be absorbed. I was terrified. I had to pick a taxi, a driver, and I didn't know what to do. There was a woman. American. Well, she was Nigerian but she had an American accent. She started shouting and waving her arms around, then guided me to a half decent looking car. She negotiated a price for me and then I was inside, my bags stowed in the boot and the driver looking smug. Like he'd won something. I don't remember talking to that woman or telling her where I wanted to go. It's like she read my mind. The driver took me straight to Dad's house in Benin. It was after lunchtime when we got there but I'd refused the offer to stop off anywhere.

Then I was standing inside Dad's compound. The earth was red and staining my trainers. It was too quiet. Like a ghost town in a Western just before something bad happens. The driver switched off his engine and when I turned to look at him, his feet were on the dashboard and he was asleep. The house looked almost new. The paint on the walls was bright and fresh but the palm nut tree was so withered it was almost a bush. The gates were gleaming in the sun and to my left the garage held what looked like a new truck. The gardens were lush and full with banana leaves and tall grass. And the chickens that mum always talked about were plump and white sitting in the hen house. White chickens made me think about the William Carlos Williams poem about red wheelbarrows and so much depending on the white chickens or something like that. It was Dia's favourite poem at school. I did look for a wheelbarrow, but there wasn't one.

The front door opened and three strangers came out. They didn't move from the steps but just stared at me. Of course, I knew they were my sisters and Ola, but they were still strangers to me. The door opened again and their mum came out and stood there. Her green and white wrapper was dirty, stained. Pulled tight across her large bosom and under her arms. Her dry feet were pushed into scruffy old slippers. The faded ribbon on the top told me they were the ones Dad had sent me shopping for years before. She began to scream. She was wailing and pulling at her grey, matted hair. The children didn't move.

When she started shouting words, I didn't understand them. They were a mixture of Pidgin and English. I didn't need to understand. The way she looked at me said it all. So if nothing happened I wouldn't have remembered all those details. I've told Dia all of this. She said she believed me.

Dad came round the corner of the house. He stood and watched me. He looked different there. Not like my dad, the one I knew in our house. His eyes were screwed up against the glare of the sun. He was dressed in an agbada and there were stains down his front. It looked like blood but when he brushed his hands down his top I could see it was only the earth. He looked taller than I remembered. His hair was lighter. He didn't seem to see me even though he was looking right at me. He cussed the others. Told them they were useless. He never spoke to me like that. Not ever. Ola and the others jumped at his voice, like someone had switched them on. One of the girls, Tosan I think, pushed her mum roughly towards the door. The other tried to hold on to her hands because she'd started to rip at her fleshy stomach that was sticking through the disturbed wrapper. Ola ran through the compound gates and disappeared from sight. I just stood there. My heart pumping hard. I felt cold even though sweat trickled down my spine and between my breasts.

I don't want to think about this anymore. But it's like I've put a movie on in my head and now it won't stop. This is why I avoid thinking about it. This is what makes me ill. But now I have to get to the end, to let it all play itself out.

Dad still hadn't looked at me. It's like he didn't see me. Instead he was looking at the tenants who slipped silently from their doors. The women standing together not talking. The men looking at Dad with pity. Only their children seemed to notice me. Small, brown bodies clothed in shorts or knickers and spotted with red dust. Staring at me with solemn faces. I hadn't moved since getting out of the car. I was willing my dad to acknowledge me. I said, 'Dad?' My voice sounded different to me. Unsure. I don't know if I said the word out loud.

'Dad, it's me.'

It felt like the tenants held a collective breath waiting to see what happened next. As though I was part of a crazy show that was going on. Dad walked around the side of the house. Away from me. He didn't even glance in my direction. I didn't know what to do.

A woman tenant walked towards me. She was talking to me. I couldn't focus my eyes on her face.

She dipped a curtsey and my mouth smiled. Other tenants came forward, patting, do-ing. The toddlers picked up on the excitement and began to push each other, tripping and laughing. I wanted to get away from them all. I was waiting for Dad to reappear. The driver was leaning out of his window not wanting to miss anything. I turned and told him to take me to a hotel.

In the car the driver started to call me sistah. He wanted information to brag and spread about to the other drivers. We turned slowly in the compound. He shouted at the children who were still running around and laughing.

Then we were on the road and his voice was louder, chatting non-stop. I stayed silent but he didn't take the hint. I tried to blend into his stained tiger-print covers and stop existing. My headache got so bad I thought my head would explode all over his seats. On the highway, traders were hustling. Gala bars, water, Fanta. No thoughts of safety as they ran between vehicles. There were children with quick looks and wide grins. It's like there were no rules. But there must be. There's always got to be rules. We inched forward slowly. Faces came and pressed up against the window, eyes trying to make contact with mine. I looked down at my hands until we drove through the hotel gates. He was still talking at me. I paid him and turned away. Even though I ignored him through the whole journey, he still got out and dragged my cases from his boot.

From the outside the hotel seemed fine. The walls were painted white and there was a glass porch leading to the reception. Potted palms lined the short walkway. A handwritten sign taped to the wall offered air conditioning. The girl on reception was sullen. I asked how much and she passed me a card displaying the rates. I can still see her face so clearly. Thin, her makeup matching skin tone perfectly, but creating a dull mask. Her orange lipstick on pouty lips hid her chipped front teeth. A perfect inverted V that she poked her tongue through when she was writing my details.

The room was okay. A large bed took up most of the space. At the foot of it a dark wood cabinet housed the wardrobe, a small TV and a mini fridge. The bathroom was clean but the shower curtain hanging from the rusting ceiling pole was thick plastic that may once have been white but had turned cream with brown water stains along the bottom. I lay down on the bed and closed my eyes.

Kutes

Me mums well off her bonce now an it aint like we knew him that much an I dont understand why weve gotta feel shit cos I dont an me nan dont either from the way shes actin and ive got me own stuff to deal with innit

im checkin on me nan everyday an then I come home an im checkin on me mum an shes like actin really weird an we should just be packin now an movin but me nans goin on about ghosts in the house an if me mum hears her goin on like that she wont want to move an I want me own flat yeah so me nan better keep it down

anyways ill still move even if me mum don't wanna itd even be better cos then I wunt have to see her everyday an me nan wud just leave me alone to get on wiv it innit

im goin out tonite I deserve it yeah an emre said hes gonna take me to that turkish restaurant in chorlton I wonder if carls can come I could like tell her to meet me there an act all surprised like shes gone in for a take away an then I can just say yeah come an eat with us least that way I wont have to put up with his tongue in me mouth after cos ill say carlys stayin at mine an then hell have to give her a lift yeah but I aint bringin carls to mine cos me mums proper on one but then if I do shell think ive just been out with carls so she wont be on me case

Ade

There are different types of fear. The exciting kind that wrapped itself around me like a brightly coloured boubou on meeting nights and then there is the other kind. I have known this since I was young. It is not something I wished on my own daughter.

I was five years old when my own sister was born. Until then I was Mama's angel. I knew that she was bringing me a sister and that I would have a responsibility. Yes, that was how Mama talked to me. I would have responsibility. Such a big word for a little girl. We knew that it would be a sister because in our family only girls are born, it is how it has been for a long time.

When I open my eyes the room is still dark. I can smell the heat sticking to my bedclothes. Funmi always comes to wake me. She is four years older than me and has been doing chores long before I wake. Mama usually follows with a candle, but today Funmi has it. Behind her a shape that is not my mama pushes through the curtain.

Aunty is standing over me, her mouth moves and says words I cannot understand. Her spit sprays on to my face. Mama never speaks to me like this, with a voice rasping like a saw on wood. I open my mouth to greet aunty properly but before I can speak her body jerks forward and she grabs at my nightgown. My mouth closes quickly. Never in all my five years have I been beaten and I fear that it is going to happen now.

'Aunty, I am sorry-o. What did I do?'

'Hnnnnh! See how it speaks, like it is my equal. I will show it.'

She is scaring me now and I shout and cry. I want Mama. Aunty pushes her hand against my mouth; her skin smells of damp earth and open fires.

Her eyes bulge and her face is close to mine. The candle that Funmi still holds in the corner of the room makes shadows over aunty's skin, making masquerade masks that alter with the movements of her lips.

'You will know what it is to suffer in your life. Do you think you are blessed like my sistah believes? Hei! Watch-o! You will suffer.'

My body shakes and as aunty pulls her hand away her long fingernail scratches my cheek. I cannot understand what I have done to evoke such hatred in her. I am scared to move as she backs away through the curtain.

I am crying loudly now. Funmi runs to me and placing the candle down carefully she takes me into her arms.

'Ade, don't tell. I beg.'

'I want Mama.'

'Ade, if you tell I will be sent away.'

This makes me cry harder because I do not want to lose Funmi. She is my big sister.

For the next two days, while Mama was in the mission hospital I stayed by Funmi's side. I did not see aunty in this time. She remained in the boy's quarters and I made sure I did not go into that part of the grounds. Normally I was not allowed out of our compound unless I was with Mama or Papa but Funmi took me everywhere. We went to the river to fetch water, to the market to barter for yam, into the hen house to collect eggs. Yes, the day my sister was born I grew up.

When Mama appeared with the baby, two days later, I had no interest in this little scrap that did nothing but scream. I had turned into a different child overnight, or so Mama told Papa. I was jealous of this baby girl. Perhaps I was spoilt and spiteful, Papa told Mama. But Funmi knew and she looked after me.

It was another two years before I found out that Funmi belonged to aunty. She was her eldest and had been born away from our village. Ma Tombe at the river was telling Ma Bunda about how aunty was a savage when they brought her home. It took three visits to the river with the clothes and Funmi before I got the full story.

Aunty was Mama's younger sister, they said. When she was born a curse was put on her by a medicine man. Heh! What a thing to tell a child. She came into the world screaming and had never stopped since, they said. This made everyone laugh loudly. Yes, she was touched, they said. Being seven or so, perhaps I was older, I did not understand what they meant, and it added to my fear of this woman who hated me.

Aunty had not been one for her lessons or learning the house so grandad arranged for her to marry young, to get her off his hands, they said. But before the ceremony, right while all the preparations were being made, after the cow and the goat had been chosen, she ran away. She took the worst boy in the village, the one with no breeding and only rags to stand up in and she disappeared, for nearly ten whole years. And when she returned it was without her husband and with Funmi trailing behind her and a baby strapped to her back.

She had learned her lesson, they said. My own mama had studied at the mission school while aunty was gone. She became a teacher and was married to Papa and had me. Mama tried to help aunty but she would not let her. She was too proud, they said. The only thing she would allow was for Funmi to work for us, but only if Mama promised to school her baby, Funmi's younger sister, as soon as she was of age. Of course, Mama agreed and that was how Funmi came to live with me.

When I heard this story I knew that Funmi was my big sister and I felt bad for her. Every time I had a lesson I would go to my room and teach Funmi. Mama gave me extra books and pencils without saying they were for Funmi. It was another one of our secrets. Life for little girls was full of them.

Elizabeth

I didn't know what to do with myself when I got to my room. I had no idea what you were supposed to do when your dad pretended you didn't exist. I went to sleep. Mum always said things were better if you slept on them.

When I woke up in that ugly hotel room I wondered whether I should go back to Dad's compound or if I should ring him. I picked up the phone next to my bed and the receptionist talked to me. I give her Dad's number and it was soon ringing.

When he answered, he said hello twice. He always answers like this, every time I ring him. I mean, rang. Not ring because obviously I can't ring him now. He never gave me a chance to respond to his first 'hello'. It pissed me off. So I was talking to him and he was acting like he didn't know me. Like he didn't know I was right there in Benin City. I was shouting at him. 'Dad I'm here, what's wrong with your wife, what's wrong with you.' But he was having a different conversation. Telling me everything's fine. Asking about Mum. I gave up. My insides started to itch. My teeth were tingling. There was a buzzing in my head. I needed to get out of the room.

Downstairs in the dining room, easy chairs formed a barrier near the door. I couldn't decide whether they were to keep people out or trap them inside. Red draylon covered in mis-matched antimacassars reminded me of old Mrs Herbert's living room. Mum took me to Mrs Herbert's when she was dying. I hated it. I must have been about ten. It smelled of old people. But standing in a stuffy dining room in Nigeria, I felt a pang of need for the familiar. I needed to be home.

I managed to calm myself down, somehow. I was hungry. After my meal I went outside and walked through the gates. The sun had dropped behind the buildings opposite. I didn't know what to do. I felt lost. I watched the cars pass by. Horns blaring, people hanging out of bus doors, wagons thundering along at breakneck speed. The smell of diesel coated my nostrils so every breath in and out tasted and smelled of the street. Wandering down to the edge of the road I became aware that I was being watched. Not only by the gateman, but by groups of lads further down the road. Turning back to the hotel I stood to one side to avoid the car that was driving through the gates. That is, until I heard my name. It was Aunty Funmi's driver. She was waiting for me. I didn't ask how she knew

I was there.

Hurrying back into the hotel, I changed quickly and grabbed my bag. When I got back downstairs the car was waiting for me, the driver standing up with the gateman smoking a brown cigarette. He flicked it away when he saw me and we climbed into the car.

On each side of the wide road, shacks were lit with kerosene lamps. They looked like fairy lights in a nativity scene. Through the open window the smell of dried fish and spices replaced the heavy diesel. Women were sitting with their piles of yam, garri, or fried fish in their laps. Their children waved at the cars, beckoning customers.

The driver was showing off or he was crazy. We took a sharp left into what looked like little more than an alleyway. He quickly manoeuvred the vehicle around potholes. I was thrown from side to side. We moved further from the highway and plunged into absolute darkness as the headlights flickered off for a second. I began thinking that I was mistaken and he wasn't from aunty after all. That he was going to take me somewhere and kill me. The driver hit the dashboard and the dimmed headlights picked out more unevenness. Another sharp left took us down a winding dirt path. The bottom of the car scraped along the road as potholes turned to craters. Finally, when I thought I couldn't take any more, we reached the wooden gates to a compound. I was ready to start crying. I was so stupid to go off with someone I didn't know.

Inside aunty was waiting. She was chuckling and pulling at me. Asking me about London. I told her I lived in Manchester. She ignored me. She'd aged but still looked like the woman who sat me on her knee when I was ten and told me stories about 'home'. I hadn't been to that house before but it felt familiar. Pictures of her daughter covered the large sideboard. Smiling, successful, married and happy. And there was a picture of me. Half of the image had faded. The scroll clasped tightly in my hand was crushed on one side. My graduation gown was lopsided.

When she'd calmed down and we were sitting together at the big kitchen table, I told her about what had happened. About Dad ignoring me. She turned serious. I didn't understand what she was saying. The Oracle. Juju. Curses. The Family. None of it made any sense. She talked for ages and I just looked at her. Panic rising and falling as I believed and disbelieved her. I can't even remember what she was saying now. But I remember how I wished I wasn't there. Hadn't climbed on the plane and decided I could just turn up uninvited.

Aunty slipped into pidgin at one point, when she got really excited.

I interrupted her, not understanding. She told me I should go home but insisted I stay with her, I'm sure she could sense my fear. The stifling heat wrapped around me. When the electricity went off I was still awake. The total silence added to my fear. Not even an insect could be heard scuttling behind the bed. My eyes adjusted. Unfamiliar shapes in the room threatened me. Taking some deep breaths, I forced my mind to empty.

At five o'clock the next morning aunty was pushing me gently on the shoulder. It was still dark outside and the naked bulb gave a dim glow to the room. I had a headache. The wrapper I slept in was damp where it stuck to my body, trapping me like a funeral shroud.

I had a bath using the bucket and bowl. The water was deliciously cold. Through the open window I could hear the driver talking, it sounded loud on the early morning air. Aunty had prepared boiled yam and fried eggs for breakfast. I didn't want to eat but forced a few mouthfuls. The tea was strong and dark, I asked for water instead. Hurrying me outside, she held me close and kissed me on both cheeks. My suitcase was on the back seat. The driver backed slowly through the gates.

The journey to the airport was bumpy and appeared to pass quickly despite it taking longer than four hours at that time. The road was quiet. Only one roadblock and the driver pushed a ten Naira note into the policeman's hand. When we reached Lagos the roads were busier. Young boys were running alongside the vehicles holding out DVDs, cheap watches, fake designer sunglasses and belts. The driver waved them out of the way as they advanced on us. At the airport he dropped me on the lower road.

Luckily, I had an open airline ticket. Two thousand Naira removed any obstacles that would stop me getting on the next plane to Manchester. There was only one hour to wait, it wasn't like it is now. You could rock up at an airport then and jump on a plane. In the departure lounge I was tempted to ring Dad again. My insides were still itching. I think I got on the plane, found my seat and slept the whole way home. Well, I'm not sure, but I can't remember anything about the trip. Except Miles Davies. On the radio. Intricate disorder soothing my insides.

When I got home I tried ringing Dad again. I wanted to know why he couldn't see me. He still acted as though I was never there. I hated him. I started to count. So no matter what Dia says, why would I remember that kind of detail if nothing happened? It doesn't make sense. It wouldn't have stayed with me like that for nearly twenty years otherwise. What if I go back there and things happen again? Maybe Dad's not really dead and he's just ignoring us. That's a possibility, isn't it? Of course it's not a possibility. My dad's dead.

Kutes

I am so gonna lose it if we dont get outta here soon me mums proper on one an ive got an essay due in an it aint even funny

most of the time me grandad was a loser period an he had to go an die an make my life harder innit why cant me mum just be normal bout it all it aint like he was anythin to us he was just a sperm donor jeez

am I the only one here who remembers shit he was all out for himself the only times we heard from him was when he wanted summat an then me mum an nan would get together and discuss it an decide that they cudnt or shudnt help him an then me nan would send me to the postoffice with a letter an me mum would be secretly sending shit an they was both pretendin that they werent doin nothin

it aint fair ive got a life too innit an noones givin a shit bout that if I dint have me mates and emre itd be like I don't exist I swear I cant wait to move out an do me own thing

Ade

That woman did not stop with her badness. Aunty was wicked, with her roots and rituals. Always she had her rituals that took her into the bush. I cannot remember how it happened on the day Funmi and I followed her. I do not know whether we did follow her or she followed us. Perhaps it was neither. Perhaps she was not even there.

It was at the beginning of rainy season, when rain seems to appear from nowhere, without any warning, and disappear just as quickly. I must have been fourteen or fifteen years old. Or maybe I was older. So long ago, I don't remember exactly. I cannot recall why we chose the bush instead of the river behind the compound. Life had become more complicated by then, we could not speak as freely as we once had. Besida and Wumi, our sisters, often came upon us by the river as they began to explore more.

That one day, when we went into the bush it disturbed our world. We were gossiping and laughing, as young girls do. We did not take notice of how deep inside the trees we travelled.

The earth smells fresh and new, full of the possibilities and life that the rains bring.

'I have decided I will marry him, Funmi.'

'Is it so? And have you decided when he will ask you?'

'Of course, it will happen after my sixteenth birthday.'

'Really? And have you decided how he will ask you?'

I look into her eyes and we begin to laugh. She knows me better than my own mama does. I open my mouth to answer but Funmi's hand on my arm stops me before I can begin. Her eyes are large and full of fear. I can hear noises, sounds that I have not heard before, but they seem familiar to Funmi. She begins to back away, holding on to my arm, pulling me with her. But I shake her off. I want to see who is making this sound. Ayaaaaaah! Ehhhhm! Eyaaaaah! Ahhhhhhn! I creep forward and sense that Funmi has stopped her retreat. I stand behind an Iroko tree wide enough to hide two of me and I lean my palms against its trunk and breathe in its scent.

The noises continue and I slowly move my head to the left of the tree. There are bushes in front of me and I have to crouch down, slowly-slowly, until I can see through a gap in the thick leaves and foliage.

I peek through. My armpits are oozing with fear. I see a creature that looks like aunty somehow. I want to pull back, to hide my face. It is doing things, strange things. Holding cloth and pencils. Chanting. I think I see my own blue pencil; the one James gave to me. And Mama's favourite house wrapper that was missing from the last wash.

I cannot move and my head begins to prickle, so that my scalp feels as though it is rising from me. I look again into the eyes and still they are staring at me, but I realise not seeing me. I move slowly behind the tree and rest my head against the bark. It feels as though night has fallen.

Funmi is beside me. She leads me away to the sound of a chicken struggling, like they do when we do not kill them cleanly. It is crowing and its wings are flapping and I imagine it is coming after me. The chants are getting louder and louder. Then silence.

At the river we sit, not speaking but holding each other. Once I have stopped shaking and my breathing returns to normal, Funmi releases me.

'It is nothing, Ade. Truly, it is nothing.'

'How can you say that Funmi, did you not see with your own eyes?'

'There was nothing to see. You know the boys from the village like to scare us.'

I look at her. Her words do not match the fear that is still etched on her face.

'Wait here, Ade. I am coming.'

Our patch of riverbank is higher than the rest of the ground and surrounded by thick bushes. Nobody can see us from any side unless they are looking for us, but we can see everything. The earth is dry and the smells from the low river are pungent. I loosen my wrapper so that I can move my legs and draw them under my chin, hugging my arms around them. The slightest scratching to my left or right makes my heart pump hard, pwarrrrr, pwarrrrrrr! It nearly jumps from my chest. A small-small lizard is looking for dinner. While I wait for Funmi I do not want to think about what I saw. Instead I think of James and imagine what it will be like to marry him. When Funmi returns, she has her small bundle, which I have seen many times before but not asked about. Carefully she places it on the ground between us. It is cotton and was once rich colours, amber and brown and black, but is now faded. She unties it and takes things out. I am shocked because I did not know that she carries fetish. Picking up each item she gives them gentle touches and strokes. I cannot say if she is reassuring them or herself. She picks up one smooth stone. I think it must be from the river it is so smooth and flat. She holds it in the palm of one hand and covers it with the other, then closes her eyes. When she has finished she places it in the centre of my hand.

Funmi's eyes are so sincere and so full of love. As she places it on my palm I can feel heat moving into my flesh. She places my other hand on top then holds them with her own. The world starts to vibrate around and within me, us. My stomach feels swelled up and the feeling spreads throughout all of my person. I feel light, as though I am the wind that blows in from the river or the bird that hovers above the mango tree. I am free and floating and for a time I do not know who I am. I am everyone and everything. It is very wonderful to experience. And I do not believe that Funmi spoke to me, but in that short time she told me everything. Somewhere I have that stone. Somewhere. I will find it and put it in my box when I am packing.

Elizabeth

I feel as though I'm stuck in another world. Dia is being sweet but it doesn't help, especially because I have to get up early and pretend I've slept on the couch. I'm tired.

The post. Four letters. Rubbish, rubbish, phone bill, what's this? Finally, the tenants have signed the agreement, which means they're moving in as soon as we move out. In six days we'll be living back at Mum's and there'll be tenants in this house and everything will be fine.

This was Dad's house. He didn't want me to live here. Or maybe he did. Maybe it's his way of doing something nice without being seen to do it. I've never thought about it like that. Maybe my dad was okay and it's because Mum was always saying to him that he couldn't do anything right that he pretended to be hard. If it was like that it means he bought the house for us to live in and I never really said thank you. He did complain about the flat we lived in before, but we liked it. There was nothing wrong with it at all and the tower blocks were better at that time. Or maybe when you're younger you don't feel it. But Dad didn't like it.

Now I'm wondering why I'm leaving. It's like Mum's house doesn't really let you go, which is a stupid thing to say but it's true. It's like it breathes and moves and stretches and contracts around everything that's going on. Or it could be that it's the one place that hasn't changed. It's always there. Mum's always there.

Ola's room feels sad now it's all packed up. Why hasn't he phoned to tell me what's happening? The curtains need to be washed. Maybe I should do all the upstairs curtains together. I'll have to wake Kutes. She's in a really bad mood at the moment. I don't know what's wrong with her. Why does she have to start with her moods now? At her age I was working at weekends. Somebody's ringing.

It's Ola. The usual pleasantries, then:

'Ola, what's happening?'

'Sistah Tosan sends her regards, she would like to speak to you. Hold on one moment please.'

'Ola I...'

'Hello aunty-o.'

'Err, hi Tosan. Are you well? Is everything okay?'

Why the hell is she laughing? I can't stand it.

'Yes, yes everyone here is fine.'

64

'Can you put Ola back on please?'

'Sistah, are you there?'

'Yes, now please tell me what's happening.'

'Don't worry, sistah. Have you thought of what you want?'

'What do you mean what I want? I just want my dad to be buried. Why can't it just get sorted out?'

'Please, sistah, calm down. Don't be upset.'

'I am not upset.'

But Kutes has put her head round the door scowling. Obviously I've been shouting.

'Hi Ola, it's Kutes here, you okay?'

'Yada yada, what's up?'

She talks to him like he's her mate, not her uncle. Why are there bits of paper under the bed? I put a bin in here for him. I don't have time for this now. There's too much to do.

Why's she shouting now?

'What?'

'I've made yer a cuppa tea's all, jeez.'

'Who are you talking to like that? I'm not your mate, I'm your mother.'

'Yeah wotever, don't know why I bother.'

'And don't think I don't know you're still sneaking around with that guy.'

'Er, sneakin don't think so that's sumthin other peeps do.'

'And what do you mean by that? Why are you starting now?'

'Did I start it tho all I did was bring you sum tea its you thats shoutin I swear I cant wait to move.'

'I wish you'd talk properly.'

Why can't she leave me alone? Who the hell is knocking on the door now?

'Elizabeth! Stop that right now and come here.'

Dia.

'Come on, hon, come and sit down. You only cleaned in here a couple of weeks ago. Come on.'

'I've got to pack, Dia. We're moving soon. I've got to get it all done.'

'Beth it's okay. Have you got a tissue?'

And sitting here on the bed wrapped up in Dia makes it better. And my yellow-gloved hands look so funny next to her smooth black fingers.

'What's so funny, huh? Ah, the gloves. Take them off and give me a proper hug.'

I can't remember why I was in such a state in the first place. I love Dia. Curtains washed and hung out, all three of us walk round to my mum's. It's a bright blue sky and fake sunshine, as Ola calls it. I don't count. Dia and Kutes are like a couple of kids the way they mess around, but I really don't mind today. When we turn the corner of Manley Road there's an old man ahead. He's wearing a Fedora and using a wooden walking stick and my heart jumps because I'm sure it's my dad. Kutes and Dia have stopped next to me. Dia touches my arm. 'What's up, love?'

But I can't move. When Dia stands in front of me I move my eyes to her face. 'That man there, he looks like...'

'What man, Mum? There's no-one else around, it's too friggin' cold to be out.'

And she's right. When I look around Dia's left shoulder the pavement's empty. Damn, I must be going mad.

Mum's got a pan on as usual. Jolloff rice by the smell of it. She looks old and small. Maybe I should have called round more often.

'Are you all right, Mum?'

'Eh-heh! Now you can ask? Perhaps you should go and check upstairs and see if the rooms are all right. Bang, bang, bang. It is a wonder a person can think-o.'

'But I told you they had to do some work. I'm sure it wasn't that bad.'

Kutes is clattering around upstairs. Dia catches my eye and her look warns me not to say anything else.

'Let's go and have a look, then. You've told me enough about it.'

Dia is good at keeping things calm.

'Won't be a minute, Mum. I'll just show Dia around.'

'Hmmmph!'

The floor tiles need a bit of a clean and that old mirror stand is looking ugly.

'The stair carpet's being fitted on Wednesday. I need to buy a shoe rack to put behind the door. I'm not having mud on the new carpets.'

The banister's smooth and warm. The wood's dark and the varnish is worn dull and smooth.

'Remember when we used to slide down it, Beth. In fact, there's where we scratched in our initials. Your mum never did find out.'

And she's right. I'd forgotten about that. We chose the bit where the banister meets the wall and marked it right underneath.

I have the two rooms on the left. The largest is my living room-cum-kitchen. There's a kitchen further along the landing but I don't want to use that one. That can be for Kutes and Ola. The two big sash windows look out on to the garden. The nest in the bare oak tree at the bottom looks bigger. I'm sure it will be magpies. They're bad luck. Well, one is bad luck. They're also too loud. Good job I got the double glazing screens.

'Are you sure this is what you want, Beth?'

'Dia, don't start again.'

'What about direct payments? Your mum could get someone to come in and help her.'

'Oh, and are you going to be the one who tells my mum she needs some help? She thinks I'm coming back because I can't cope.'

'I was just saying. Let's go up and see Kutes' room.'

'Come and check the bedroom first.'

The hallway is darker after the brightness of my living room. The wardrobes that have been built in are perfect. I've closed off the door to the bathroom from the hallway and made it en-suite.

'So what do you think, Dia? Do you like it?'

'It's lovely, Beth. Really.'

Kicking the door closed, she gets hold of me and pulls me up close against her. The buckle of her belt digs into my stomach and I press closer still. We kiss and I pull away. Dia laughs. Kutes is banging around upstairs. It sounds like she's dancing or jogging on the spot. I hope her room's okay. We leave the bedroom and go upstairs.

'What do you think, Kutes? Do you like it?'

'It's all right.'

Pointless talking to her really. Back downstairs Mum has laid the table.

'Upstairs looks lovely, mum.'

'Is it so? With all the noise and banging that I have had to listen to it is a wonder we have any rooms left.'

'Sorry.'

'It is done now. So sit. You have not been eating properly.'

Kutes

hey carls are ya there
    yeah yeah u ok hon
    me mums a rite bitch
    Wot u done now
    I was breathin dunt have to be more than that
    haha yer crazy
    anyways when I was packin i found all these dam ugly baby pics an i
think me dads in one of em
        yer dad as a ugly baby??????
    haha don't be a dick no hes holdin me
    thort u dint no yer dad
    der i don't do i so it means me mums bin lyin innit
    o shit so wots she sed
    she aint sed nuthin thats the prob innit she used to get all upset wen I
asked her bout im so I stopped cos I dint wanna no if she was like ya no
forced or summat
        yeah but even if uve got a rite to no innit wots he look like anyways
        dunno i can only see his hand an his leg
        well it mite not be him then
        it is i no it is an that means there mite be otha pics of him
        so wot u gonna do
        dunno yet
        well it aint like ur a kid so just tell yer mum u wanna no about him
        it aint that easy though is it cos shes off her tree
        nah she cant be that bad
        yeah if yer mums normal that is
        so wots yer new house like
        me rooms wicked its like a proper bedsit
        cool will yer be able to sneak emre in then haha
        nah no chance gotta get past me nan an me mum an me anty dia if shes
around so that aint happenin
        he wont be happy bout that then
        woteva im not arsed it aint like hes taken me to his anyways not that I
wanna go but he cant say nuthin then can he
        you still aint been to his I thought he was takin you there last week he
is so married i swear down

no he aint id no if he was married he asked me to move in with him
innit

what??????? And you dint think to tell me

well I weren't gonna do it was I but now I might I swear down it'll be
serves her right

no fucking way kutes I wont let you jeezus we need a serious talk girl

wotevs im gonna pack some more laters

Ade

Heh! You become older in your body but your mind, it goes backwards. So many things to prepare for my trip. I will write a list, Kutes will shop for me. We will stay in Lagos first. At Funmi's daughter's house. It is good that she married a Lagos man, a big man who has treated her well. It is a shame that my Elizabeth did not find such a man. But she has those funny ways so there is no use thinking about that.

Heh! The letters Funmi wrote to me when our daughter was to marry. And I bought the finest cloth from Taylor Barrett. Right here in Manchester. Can you imagine? Yards and yards of gold and white organza of the best cotton. African cotton. I have the photographs somewhere here. Somewhere.

Only one daughter Funmi had. So much sadness as babies fell from her womb each year just like my own. Until her husband forbade her to travel to the village. Someone did not wish her well and her husband forbade her from returning. She was very unhappy until her daughter came-o. The wedding was beautiful. My Elizabeth was only ten years old. So many questions she asked me about Africa. Elephants and lions in the street. Hah! What were they teaching our children at school?

It was the first time I had travelled by plane. It was my first trip home. Out of exile, just like the Presidents who leave their own people after a coup. More than thirty years I had been gone and so many changes had taken place. But the wedding was beautiful. Three whole days of celebration, done Lagos style even though it was held in our village.

That village was almost a town when I went back. I had received many letters from Funmi and had known about each new compound and timber yard and workshop and market that was attaching itself, yet until then I never saw my village as any different than when I had left. Such sadness because both Mama and Papa were not there. But the wedding was very beautiful. Two cows were cooked. Our daughter was marrying a big man in Lagos. I cannot remember what his job was but I know it was big-big.

Ahhh, too many memories. Sometimes I think I have not done such a good job in raising Elizabeth. She has very funny ideas about what is right and good. I should have returned home with my husband and she would not be so foo-foo, sha! But what am I saying. I did not have a home by then. Mama and Papa had both gone. It is enough. Kutes will shop for me.

Elizabeth

My dad's dead and I don't feel anything. There were times when I wished he'd never been my dad. He upset me more times than he made me happy, the few times I saw him. I wasn't tall enough, dark enough, clever enough. Even when I did my degree it wasn't the right kind. I should have read law or studied medicine, he said. I went to the local comprehensive, how the hell was I supposed to be a doctor?

I tried to tell Kutes that this morning. When she was asking about him. But she got in a strop again. He was ordinary. His mum was ordinary. Their council house was ordinary. His mum told me how he ran around doing jobs for people, earning pennies, taking home black market cigarettes.

The first time he took me to see her I must have been about seven or eight. She lived on a bit of a posh estate back then. I suppose it would be a housing association estate now, but back then it was a step up from a council estate. All the houses had thick privets at the front and a green metal gate. The garden was huge and messy and there was a ginnel at the side. There were bits of bicycles all over the front garden. Handle bars, a chopper seat, one pedal. It was Dad's brother, who was a bit slow according to Mum. He tried to fix things. I wanted a chopper bike like my friends at school and Mum wouldn't even get me a second hand girl's bike. The front door was dirty and looked like it had been gouged at one side. It was red and I thought it should have been green like the gate.

She was so wrinkled and old and she had a hacking cough. She sounded like a blocked plughole when she breathed. There were dog hairs on everything and a German Shepherd in a basket in the corner that looked older than her. It was bloody awful. She didn't even talk to me and she was horrible to my dad. He was just as horrible back. I couldn't breathe so I asked if I could go in the back garden. It stunk of dog shit. I stood in the ginnel counting the Mackeson bottles lined up against the wall until my dad came out. I didn't say goodbye but I think I heard her shout something about a half-breed through the kitchen window and I thought she was talking about the dog.

When we arrived home Dad was in a mood. I watched TV as Mum argued with him for ages.

Kutes

she is so out of order she new exactly what I was sayin an then she starts goin on about her dad like shes the only one who has one an I know she was tryin to make out like dads are not all that but at the end of the day if I dint have one I wouldnt be here

im sick of having to creep around her all the time cos shes so effin delicate it aint fair all I says is I found a picture yeah an I thought it was me dad an she starts on about her dad like me an her is one or summat an it aint right howm I supposed to feel

an then if I goes to me nan she aint telling me shit cos I tried that last week an then she starts goin on about her own dad an its like they don't know I exist it aint fair im so goin out tonight an im gettin trashed ive had enough

Ade

So many changes are happening. Has it not always been so? The first time I became aware of what change could do, I was hiding behind the hen house. The compound was dark except for the lantern set inside the circle of men. Leaning my head against the rough wood I waited for the talking to begin. The hens were snuffling in their beds and the smell of them seeped through the cracks in the wood. Responsibility for the hens had passed over to my small sister, Wumi. Mama had about twenty-five plump white hens. Wumi was not as careful as I had been. Many times she broke more eggs than she collected. I had shown her how to lean right over. To scoop upwards beneath the egg and cradle it in her palm. I missed the hens.

There is more movement with the group of men and I peep around the corner. It is James. Light is bouncing off his face as he takes his seat on the log beside Uncle Tunde. Papa bangs his stick on the earth and intones for the blessings of our ancestors. He passes round a plate and I know it is kola nut and that palm wine will follow before the meeting begins. I rest my head back against the hut while I wait. This part can take a long time. James did not chew his kola nut. He passed his hand over his mouth but I saw him drop the nut inside his shirt pocket. His mouth must not be able to take the bitterness. I like to think about James's mouth. I like to imagine what it is like to kiss.

A thick, heavy, warm darkness hangs over the compound for as far as I can see. I hear a faint noise ahead of me and hold my breath. Seconds later Funmi flops down beside me. Mama says she is like a cat, she can see through the dark. We put our heads close together and giggle into our hands.

Papa is pouring libation on to the floor.

Once the men start talking, Funmi and I lie on our stomachs in the grass and try to hear what they are saying. She puts her mouth against my ear and whispers, 'look-o, your own man looks like a pale god.' Her breath tickles me and makes shivers run down my back. I pinch her arm gently. We have to be so quiet. Papa would beat us if he found us.

The meeting is very long. The grass is scratching my stomach and sticking into my chin. Mosquitos, zzzz-zzzz-zzzz in my ear looking for blood. It is everything I can do to remain still. Occasionally Papa raises his voice, explaining how he does not want to rush. That much time is needed to prepare for our future. That war brings opportunity. James's voice is low but persuasive because every time he speaks there are grunts of approval from all the men. My heart swells with pride for him.

James is the last to leave and I am sure that he looks straight at me. Lying there with Funmi by my side breathing gently in her sleep. I see him look at me before he turns his back. That would not have been possible. The only light came from the lantern, which had burned low and the pool of light did not reach the corner of the hen house. Shaking Funmi awake we wait until Papa lifts the lantern and turns the corner on his way to the compound gates with James. If we do not hurry we will be locked out for the night. Bending low with the hot darkness as cover, Funmi leads me to the back door. We dust our feet as best we can before creeping along the passageway and pushing the heavy curtain to my room aside. We sleep together in my bed where I dream about the white man's war and bombs like great vultures hovering over our compound.

The next morning after our chores, Funmi and I went down to the part of the river that ran behind our compound. I told her that the whole world was at war. But she laughed at me. She did not take me seriously. After all, in our world we were not at war. Of course, she was right, so I tried to recall all the plans that I had heard. That while the British were busy our people could rise up in their businesses. Our father could manage, and own, and decide and make more money than before. Everyone could work and share what had been taken away. Papa had been reluctant to agree but James had persuaded him and Uncle Tunde to join into the union properly. Funmi and I discussed in great detail what this union could be and how it would help us all if it made Mama sad and could only be discussed in the dark night.

Later in the evening while I was cooking with Mama, I asked her about the white man's war. She was vexed and told me it was not my business. And the world war did become our concern. Papa was away from our compound much more often. And when he was home, he and Mama hardly spoke, except to discuss my sister and myself. Mama was sad and Papa's secrets stuck to him like gum from the tree and attracted people who would come to him and talk in low earnest voices.

I became frightened of what would happen, and even though I went to school each day and taught Funmi my lessons, and walked to the river, and greeted the neighbours as usual, something was changing.

Elizabeth

'Beth, why are you standing in the middle of the living room? You need to let them get on with it.'

'But I need to clean here. The tenants are moving in tomorrow.'

'You've cleaned every inch of this house.'

'Jeez mum, is that all you can go on about?'

'Don't be cheeky to your mum, Kutes, go and make sure you've got everything.'

It's all difficult enough without her attitude. If Dia hadn't taken the day off I wouldn't be able to cope.

'Hello, earth to Beth. Are you with us?'

'Dia, I don't know what I'd do without you.'

'Right, I'm going over to your mum's house so I'll be there when they arrive. I'll take Kutes.'

I should have rung Ola before the phone was switched over. Shit. Now he won't have my number and it's too expensive to call the mobile. Shit. Shit. Shit. I hope I'm doing the right thing. But it's a bit late if I'm not. What the hell am I going on about? Concentrate. That guy is getting on my last nerve with his whistling. Why do workmen whistle? Surely it's a myth. But he's doing it. And he stinks of sweat and it's not like it's hot, it's bloody November. Ah, they're going.

The house feels so different now. I hope the tenants look after it. But it's only a six-month contract so they can't do much damage in that time. And it's unfurnished so it's not like they're using my stuff. Dia says I have to think about where I'm living and not what's happening here. It's easy for her to say with her meditating and aura of zen.

Kutes

'Nah, I swear Aunty Dia shes well out of order. I dint even tell you what shes been going on with. It aint fair cos I only asked about a photo I found and she gave it to me in me baby book so its not like I was snooping around an then she wont tell me if its me dad and it aint fair.'

'Whoa, Kutes. Take a breath. What are you talking about?'

'I'm talking about my dad and I was tryin to ask her about him and she just went on about her own dad and then I tried to ask me nan an she was going on about hers. Its like I don't exist'

'Don't be like that, hon. You know your mum's stressed, with her dad dying and moving house. And your nana's old, she's got enough to deal with. Just wait a while and have another talk to her when things settle down.'

'Why do I always have to wait? It aint fair. You know who he is dont you? Why dont you tell me then I'll leave her alone?'

'Kutes, this really isn't the time. Why haven't you had this conversation with your mum before? Why do you have to bring it up right now, when she's trying to cope with other stuff?'

'Woteva, see you're doin it as well. I aint askin anyone anythin, I dont friggin care.'

Ade

Heh! What a rumpus. I cannot believe it is possible to make so much noise. There has been a breeze blowing through my rooms all morning. Men, grunting and whistling I could not hear the television set properly. It is the wooden floors. Elizabeth is insisting that she does not have carpet. How times have changed. Now it is modern to have less. To live with wooden floorboards.

Perhaps it was not such a good idea to share my home once more. I have become accustomed to my quietness. Ah, but it was not always so quiet. We had many parties in this very room. For every excuse: birth, naming ceremony, marriage, divorce and death. When I was young we partied. Food and music, dancing into the night. I suppose because we were all young together. Some of my boarders were older than me in fact and introduced me to many new things. Dances from back home that I had not seen before. Yes, there were many happy times in this house. Even with James at the beginning. Is this not where we lived together? Is this not where Elizabeth was born? There was a time when James and I could not wait for parties to end and for people to leave our rooms. I was young once. We would look at each other across the room or he would pass behind me while I was serving food and whisper my name. But what am I thinking?

It is right that my children come home. And perhaps it is now time for me to think of going back. We will go and lay my husband to rest. It does not seem so long ago that James and I were travelling here. It is as though years have been stolen when I was not looking.

Elizabeth

I met Femi here, right here in this room. I was twenty-six. I shouldn't have been living at home. But I was. My mind had been ill too long. It scared me. The only reason I knew I wasn't actually full blown crazy was because I kept asking if I was going crazy. Therapists, medications, a week in a 'resting' unit. Was that really me? Did that actually happen? My mind let me down so badly. Nearly two years of my life taken away. I'd eventually finished university and was thinking about what to do next. I considered teaching but didn't know if I liked children enough and my medical records weren't best suited to being in a classroom if I'm honest.

I felt as though I knew him, Femi. He'd come to stay with us because mum was still letting out rooms to students. Well, that's what I thought at the time but it works out she knew his dad from years back, when she first came. She hadn't said that when he moved in, though. Or maybe she did and I didn't listen. They'd come up from London. His dad drove a black Granada. It was so highly polished, it looked like it was never used. The chrome bits were gleaming and even while Femi was moving his stuff in, his dad had a cloth out, wiping the bumpers and the light casings. I think his dad stayed around for a few days. I'm sure of it. I saw him coming out of mum's bathroom one night when I came home. Mum was all giggly and daft and I hardly saw her. Yes, that's right. I was thinking about moving out. She wasn't around. Why am I remembering that now? I'm not really interested in what my mum was doing with some uncle.

Femi was at UMIST doing his masters in structural engineering. He looked like my picture of Huey P Newton. The one where he's got his top off. I don't know where that went. Maybe I didn't have a picture. Maybe it was in the books and stuff we were reading then. It was coming to the end of the Black Panther movement I'm sure, because Dia had stopped wearing that black beret all the time. We were still going to African awareness classes though. Well Dia was, I was more than aware of Africa. Maybe I'm wrong though because why else would Femi have reminded me of Newton? I was living upstairs, in what's Kutes' room now, when he moved in here. I was getting better. I didn't see him much. He was always studying or working, but I spied on him. I could bump into him accidentally any time he came out of his room. Three years and two months older than me and he was tall enough for me to look up at him. I knew he was engaged. Mum treated him like a son, but I didn't want a brother.

Sometimes, when we weren't at meetings, we'd go out with the other postgraduates that lived in the rooms. But I wasn't interested in what anybody had to say, really. I would wait for Femi to notice me, touch my arm, smile at me. And I wasn't the only one. There was one woman, she wasn't even African, but she was always there. I convinced myself he couldn't like her. After all, he was engaged. But they got on and I hated her.

The Grants Arms in Hulme was our favourite place. We'd sit in the corner and discuss politics. It was different to the other meetings that Dia and I went to. This was more about communism and there were loads of different people involved, white and black. Always going on about demonstrations and it bored me senseless. They weren't telling me anything new, it's all I'd heard when I was growing up. It was romantic though in some ways. There was always so much happening.

One time, we were all at a rally at the Hippodrome. I don't know what came over me. There were maybe three or four guys on the stage and they were spouting the usual comrade stuff. Not that I wasn't interested, I was. But Femi was standing in front of me and I could smell him. Brut 33. But it smelled different on him. And he had hair oil on and I could see the way his stray hairs left the rest of his head and crept down into his collar. Just a few. And I was sniffing him. Blatantly. Because there were so many people there he wouldn't know. I was miles away. I can't believe I thought like that back then.

Anyway, Dia was next to me and I heard her suck her teeth, right beside my ear. It woke me up, that and the fact she was kind of nudging me. When I glanced at her she was nodding her head towards the front of the room in a kind of 'will you look at that' way and she was pulling a face so I started listening. The pasty guy who was talking was going on about some Aryan race shit and the meeting wasn't about that obviously, or we wouldn't have been there. A sudden crackle of tension around where we were standing made us tense up. A room of about one hundred and fifty people with six or seven black faces. I don't know what made me do it, but I shouted something like, 'sorry, comrade. I don't understand you. Could you speak in English, please?' Dia cracked up next to me and some guy across the room shouted, 'say it, sistah' and Femi turned around and looked into my eyes. His were laughing and I could feel the laugh right down inside of me and I swear, if it was possible, I would have been pregnant there and then.

People started pushing and jostling us and then we were somehow outside on the pavement with the doors firmly closed. We were laughing so hard I thought I might pee. Femi picked me up and swung me around. Then he did the same to Dia. There were the other black students who we didn't know and they joined in. We all piled into the Grants Arms. That was one of the best nights.

I thought I was in love for the first time and I only had six months left to make him notice me before he moved back to London and got married and I never saw him again. He'd been living in our house for more than a year and I was giving up hope. Oh, I hadn't been sitting around waiting for him. I had my friends, and we did all sorts of things besides meetings - clubbing, days out in Blackpool, we all sported Afros and platform boots. We were normal, I guess, and sometimes when we were ready for a night out in our sparkly flares and blue eye make-up we'd make so much noise when we passed his door that he'd come out and suggest he should go with us.

But it was always a girl's night out and Dia was having none of it. She'd say something funny to him that would make him laugh and go back inside. I was envious that she could do that because my mouth just stopped working when I saw him. Dia knew I was confused around him and she did everything she could to distract me. And I kind of knew why she was doing that at the time but I pretended it was because she was looking out for me. Sometimes it was like we were joined together, two opposites that needed each other to survive. I didn't know then that was real love. She'd been there when I was ill and it felt good that she always knew what to do.

Finally, he noticed me. I'd been out with the girls and for some reason they didn't come back to stay. Dia was going on holiday, I think, and Jen needed to work the next day so it was just me. I was trying to get my key in the lock of the front door, when it opened and Femi was smiling at me.

He held my arm and walked up the stairs with me, offered me a cup of tea and I was floating. The black russians I'd been drinking all night were making my head swim and I was so happy. There was nowhere to sit in his room because the chair next to his desk was covered in books and the armchair next to the heater had papers all over it. We had to sit on his bed. I made the first move. Or maybe we moved together, it doesn't matter really. We kissed and he was so sweet and gentle. He wasn't my first, of course, that had been Vernon from school, when I was eighteen.

Femi and I got together that night and I was sure he'd stay. He'd leave his fiancée and get work in Manchester and we'd be together. Not that he told me any of that. In fact, we weren't really together. I'm sure we didn't do it much after that. Or did we? We must have done... I can't remember. Anyway, when he graduated his family and his girlfriend came and I locked myself in my room for a month. He'd gone back to London by the time my morning sickness started.

I told Dia first. Well she kind of guessed. She was so pissed at me and I couldn't work out why. I probably would have been depressed for longer if she hadn't been like that though. Because suddenly, even though she was with someone, everything made sense. Dia was my person. She always had been. And she was there when I needed her and even though she was vexed she was still organising me and making sure I got vitamins and antenatal appointments. But it wasn't just her doing for me. I was there for her, too. Sometimes she was so damn moody and her girlfriends used to come and moan to me about it and then I was the one who had to check her. So it was both ways. It's just sometimes it felt like she was the one doing everything. In fact, it was Dia who dragged me downstairs to tell Mum when I was scared to.

I never told my mum who and she never asked. I'm sure she knew but she just dealt with it like she deals with everything. I don't know why I'm thinking about that now. I'll go down and see her. I haven't spoken to her properly since we moved back in.

Mum's watching an old black and white movie when I walk in. I don't think she's noticed me and I watch her for a while. Her lips are moving as though she's speaking the lines for Sophia Loren. She looks old and a little bit lost and it upsets me. There was a time when she was lively and fiery, bustling around. Now I notice there's a layer of dust along the sideboard and the table still has her cup and saucer on it from breakfast time. There's an old shoebox next to them. The one she keeps her photographs in. On top there's a picture of mum and dad. It's black and white and quite faded. They both look so young. I realise she's talking to me.

'Elizabeth, are you listening to me?'

'Sorry, Mum, what did you say?'

'I need my cases from downstairs. And Kutes must shop for me.'

'We can do it after Christmas, Mum. I haven't even booked the tickets yet. There's no rush. Are you sure you want to travel? We don't have to go.'

But of course we do and I leave the room and walk along the hallway without looking at the tiles. Upstairs, I take out the dry mop and run it over my polished floorboards.

I don't want to think about Femi. I don't want to think about my dad. I have to book tickets, but first I need to clean my bathroom The smell of bleach calms me. Then, opening my laptop, I search for flights. Air France is the cheapest. I don't know what date to book for. Do we need to be there for too long? I try a few different dates and there's little price difference. I don't want to book it yet. Maybe we won't have to go.

Kutes

I found that picture agen when I was unpackin me stuff an I dont like it it aint rite cos ive been lookin forward to tonite for weeks yeah an all I can think about is me dad well I dont even know if its me dad do I but I bet it is

an then when I was in me nans before there was these pictures yeah an me nan was goin all like memory lane on em an I swear there was one that looked like me but it couldnt have been cos it was like well old all black an white an old fashioned clothes an it werent me mum

an me nan was goin on about some guy sayin how he was really cool an shit an that means if me nan new him hed be like a hundred or summat now so theres no way me mum was shtuppin him ewwwww that's gross yer not supposed to think about them things like she ever did it

ewwwwwwwww I better stop it or I wont be goin anywhere wheres me friggin skinny jeans I cant find anythin an im seein emre so I gotta look good cos hell complain an I aint in the mood for him goin on at me tonight

Ade

The first time I did something with James was after one of Papa's meetings. We had spoken many times since the night he caught me listening. He gave Funmi a note for me, telling me to wait by the hen house. I had told her that he knew we were there and she had to believe me when we got the note.

'Did I not tell you? He is my prince.'

'But Ade, are you ready for this now - what about your papa?'

'Hei, Funmi, where is your romance. Is this not what happens in the stories?'

We finish our chores quickly and wait for Mama to retire to her room. While the meeting takes place I bathe, scrubbing my skin with Mama's best soap. Funmi pats me down with rose talcum powder and we giggle like small girls. We rub coconut oil in my hair and wrap it well. Funmi brings my orange and blue wrapper and ties it tightly.

'It must not be so easy-o, for it to come away.'

'Hah! Of course it will not be removed, he is a gentleman.'

We collapse against each other laughing to cover our anxiousness. At the back of the house, we wait for the men to stop chat-chatting. Finally they stand to leave. Funmi whispers, 'I will wait by the window.' My stomach feels like it is holding worms. James is in the light from the lantern, shaking Papa's hand, but I know he is looking straight at me.

After Papa goes and I hear the door close and the bolt being pulled across, I become scared. James has left. I am standing beside the hen house in the pitch black. Anything could happen. Has Mama not told me about egungun who hunt at night looking for innocent young girls who do not do as they are told. I am ready to fly to the door and hammer for Papa to let me in. I will take the beating as long as the egungun do not take me. Then James is behind me. His hands hold around my belly. I have never had a man so close to me so that all of his body is touching. He kisses the back of my neck and moves his hands up and down. He is pressed up against me. His breath is sharp and quick. It should not be like this. We should be whispering to each other. Holding hands and looking into each other's eyes. I turn in his arms. The night is too dark to see his eyes but I know he loves me. He is my prince. With golden hair. Without speaking to me he takes hold of my hand and leads me to the back of the compound. When we have passed the mango tree and the boy's quarters he stops, as though he is unsure of where to go. I know the old play area and lead him to the corner, behind the tall banana plants. He dares to flick his lighter so we can see the den Funmi and I built when we were young. Pushing aside the fronds we move inside and sit side by side on the old mattress.

He tickles the inside of my arm and it makes me shiver. He still has not spoken to me and he sounds out of breath. As though he has been running. I am not sure what I should do. When I turn my head to ask him he starts to kiss me on the mouth. I can smell tobacco on his moustache and it makes me want to pull away. His lips are wet. I try to think about how they look, in the daytime, when he speaks and laughs. He pushes his tongue into my mouth and it makes me choke a little. But Funmi and I have practiced kissing. We know about what happens so I try to relax.

'That's my girl,' he whispers against my mouth. He called me his girl. He is breathing faster now. He leans me back against the wall, before sliding my body sideways so that I am lying down. I feel like a woman. I begin to kiss him back and then he is on top of me and he is moving around and I cannot breathe. I try to tell him but he is moving fast-fast.

'Ade, Ade what are you doing to me? Do you like it? Tell me you like it.'

But I cannot speak because he is so heavy. He rolls off me and I take a deep breath and he guides my hand down his trouser. He curls my fingers around his thing and moves my hand up and down. He tries to move on top of me again, but I am too quick and he only rolls half on me. He is panting again and the way he is holding my hand on his thing is hurting my wrist. His body goes rigid and my hand is all wet and he is kissing me again and wrapping his arms around me. I do not know what to do with my wet hand so I hold it away from his back.

'We'll wait, Ade. Until you're sixteen, okay?'

I do not know what we will wait for but I do not say anything. It is nice to lie in his arms and feel his warm breath on my shoulder. I feel very grown up. James is a man. He is twenty-three years old and he loves me. I will wait forever if it means we will be together.

But of course there is no such thing as forever. That was a childish dream. I will not complain about anything. Did my own mama not tell me that life is fated? That we do not have a choice of what we can do. So, if I am to believe this, it is fate that my daughter has returned home. It is fate that my husband has died. And it is fate that we shall travel home.

Elizabeth

It's happened. We're going. I feel sick. It's been two months and I should be getting ready for Christmas but instead I've got to sort out injections. I have to ring Ola. Kutes took the last phone call, and she might have taken the message down wrong. He can't be buried at Christmas.

'Ola, is that you?'

'Yes, sistah, how now?'

'I'm fine, are you ok? You spoke to Kutes, what's happening?'

'We have decided to do the burial in January. Towards the end-o. What do you want us to do, sistah? For preparation.'

'I don't know. I don't know what I have to do.'

'It is the money-o. We need to make arrangements and pay for everything.'

'I told you, we're sending some money. I have to go now.'

'Ok, sis, don't worry. It will be well.'

'Bye.'

So Kutes did get it wrong, we've got six weeks to prepare. Sometimes I think I see Dad at the end of the hallway before you turn the corner to the attic stairs, and he's always got his back to me. He always wears a Fedora. I only saw him wear one once, when he came to visit. In the photographs Mum has, he wears a flat cap.

There's no family left in Manchester for my dad except us. There are sixteen stairs to the hallway. Fourteen stairs to the attic. I don't know how many there are to the cellar. I don't go into the cellar. I did when I was younger. It was a playroom. Until Dad told me there were ancestors in there, watching me.

'Mum what you standing in the hallway for? Jeez I nearly had a heart attack.'

'I'm thinking. I spoke to Ola.'

'Yeah, gotta go, I'm meeting Carls. See ya.'

She's probably meeting that guy and not Carly. She won't have tidied her room either. When I was a child I rarely came up here to the first floor. It was supposedly out of bounds, unless Dia and Jen were around and then it became a playground, but now it's mine. I'll go and tell my mum we're going to Nigeria. I want to bury my dad.

'Elizabeth, is it you? wetin you dey do? Come.'

I never hear her. Even at her age she doesn't shuffle around. Old people should shuffle. In the kitchen she's got bits of paper all over the table. And photographs.

'See this one? This one here? This is your father and myself at the Conference. On the front row.'

I can see no resemblance to the woman sitting in front of me or to the man in the fedora who walks the landing. These people are young. My dad's face stands out among the surrounding African faces. He should look out of place but he doesn't. He's leaning back against the bench, his arm flung casually over it towards my mum and his legs are crossed. He's looking up. My mum is looking at him.

'Why didn't you go back with him, Mum? Why did we have to stay here?'

'There was too much to do-o. And I had this house to attend to.'

There are letters that I haven't seen before. There's no reason I should have, I suppose. The paper is thin and crackles with age. Airmail. They're from Aunt Funmi. Mum is picking up and putting down papers and photos and mumbling to herself. I want to put them in date order, group the photographs together. She's moving them around and picking the same ones up and I have to stop myself from shouting at her. I didn't realise she was this old. I don't know when it happened.

'Are you crying, Beth?'

Apparently my tears can happen without notice. I brush my fingers over my face, start to pick up letters and begin to sort them out.

'Mum, I spoke to Ola. The funeral is on the twentieth of January. We need to get sorted out. I'll book the tickets.'

'Yes daughter, we will go one week before. I have arranged with Funmi's daughter.'

'I need to tell Kutes. Will you do it?'

'There is nothing to tell, we will all go.'

'Now see this one. This is Charles a terrible old man. Did I tell you of him?'

And I sit back and let her talk. It's only when she gets to the picture of Olu that I begin to take notice. Next to him is his wife and she's holding a child who's about two years old. When I look closely, even through the grain of the picture, I can see the likeness to Kutes and it shocks me and I wonder if my mum can see it too.

Kutes

It dunt even need to be haunted in this house cos me mums like ghost its about time she went back to work at least then I don't have to tell her everythin im doin like im gonna say yeah im off to see emre not that I am but I could be an its not her business

anyways im still not talkin to her cos me anty dia says wait for a few weeks an its been like 4 an shes still goin on with herself

carls is right I suppose it dunt really matter cos dads arent all that an if I ignore her shell leave me alone an probs not want me to go to the funeral

yay I dint think about that

Ade

One day, after I had been here for about one month, I think, maybe longer - I forget - Olu took me on a long walk to Oxford Road. It was exciting, sha! Men in uniforms walking around and people busy-busy rushing up and down that road. There was a hat shop. I decided that I would have one of those fancy hats. Olu laughed at me. 'Where you dey go to wear such a hat?' I did get one though. And I wore it.

He stopped at one shop on Oxford Road and opened the door. Inside there were many African faces and they turned around and looked at us as we walked in. It is strange for me to think in this manner. But that is how it was when I first arrived. We stood out. It did not take too long for me to begin noticing African people in Manchester. At home I had only noticed the white man. I hid behind Olu. One man came from the back and shook hands with us, though he had to wait for me to take off my gloves. I do not remember what we said to each other but I do remember that he laughed at me. It seemed that good manners were something not required in Mr Konnen's eating place.

Olu bought us some drinks and we sat down at a table near to the back of the shop. It was a restaurant that Mr Konnen had set up and where the coloured American soldiers could relax. Olu explained to me that they could not go to other places very easily but here they could drink and eat food from home and even dance in the evenings. Since the war was over now there were less soldiers around but still the room was very busy.

While I looked around and read the posters for Bovril and Camp Coffee that were on the walls, Olu and the man talked quietly. They were discussing about one man from America who was coming to visit them soon but their voices mingled with all the other voices and I did not pay them much attention. When we got up to leave, my drink, which had tasted very sweet like mango, had been finished for a long time. My eyes were itching, as though I had been leaning too close to the fire while cooking. The air was thick. So many people were smoking cigarettes.

Olu told me that he had secured some work for me. I had my first job in Manchester serving the tables and washing up at the enormous sink in the back. I was excited to return home and tell Mrs Kingsley. I had been helping her with the cleaning, not because I enjoyed this but because I needed something to fill my time. The next time James arrived to see me, he was very cheerful and made jokes with Mrs Kingsley, telling her how she looked beautiful. This is just how Papa would tease Mama when he had been away for longer than he said, or when he had been drinking too much palm wine.

He told me to collect my coat so that we could go out for a walk. I did not feel to tell him that I went out to the park often with Olu. Instead I ran up those stairs. Yes, I was happy to run up and down the stairs by that point, sha! I had something to tell James and the walk would be a good time to do it. Did I think I would get the time to talk-o? James tucked my arm into his and began to tell me how busy he had been. Meetings. For three weeks, sha! He talked and talked about going here and there. I could not get one word out of my mouth. When we reached the end of the park I told him quickly that I had a job. I was excited. I wanted him to be pleased.

Ah! You would think I have told him that I am planning to ride to the moon. You would think that Olu is the devil.

'What do you mean you've been out with that fella?'

'It is Olu, James, is he not my own brother?'

'No, Ade, he is not your own brother, he is a bloody man and he only wants one bloody thing from you.'

I believed him to be having a joke with me so I laughed.

'I don't think it's funny, Ade. What would your mother say? She'd beat you that's what she'd do. Running around the streets with a man you don't know.'

'Yes-o James, but she would hug me for running away with you, isn't it?'

'We're not talking about me. I don't want you seeing him. You don't know anything about him. Where's he even from.'

'He is from home and he has been to see me when you have not been near.'

'How many times? What have you been saying to him? You know you can get me in trouble.'

'Why would you be in trouble? Am I not old enough to travel?'

'What have you told him, Ade?'

'Nothing. I have not spoken to him about you. I did not wish to embarrass myself when he asked where you were, why you had not visited me in all this time.'

I have not seen James behave in this manner before and I do not like it. He would not have dared to speak to me like this in my mama's compound. We continue to walk around the park but my heart has gone back to my room. James is very gloomy and stamps his feet as he walks with his big steps. I have to run to keep up with him, sha! When we approach a bench I take my arm from his and sit down. I refuse to walk one more step with him. He will not turn around and look at me so I talk at his big back.

'I am going to work for Mr Konnen in his restaurant, if you are interested. And I will begin this Saturday.'

James turns round with a smile on his face. He comes and sits next to me and picks up my hand, rubbing it in between both of his.

'I was worried, Ade, that's all. Let's not fight.'

'Was it not you who fought me? You would not allow me to speak.'

'Forget that now. I've got to look after you, it's the least I can do.'

Hei! This James makes my heart melt. I cannot stay vexed with him for long when he smiles at me like this.

'So have you met Mr Konnen then? What's he like? I was thinking of popping in to see him, so I'll take you tomorrow.'

A woman who has been watching us from the edge of the pond approaches and looks directly at James. She has a woollen coat on that pinches in at her waist, and I'm sure she has stockings on. It is a pity about the scarf that is tied around her head, a hat would be better. I want a coat like that one. It seems she does not notice me though, even when I smile. But she opens her mouth-o! Heh! Looking so fine and speaking like a common workman. Of course, I do not understand everything she says because her accent is very strong. James replies to her in the same way then drags me up by my arm and walks us quickly away. He does not explain what has happened but I know.

This photograph was taken around that time. We were very young. I had yet to learn many things.

Elizabeth

When I was younger I pretended that I had another dad, one who lived close by. I wanted to be normal. Like Dia and Jen. I was lopsided. They loved coming here to our house and playing in the corridors and the attic when there were no students living in it. I loved going to Dia's cosy terraced house with small rooms and no places to hide.

I saw him again last night. I was rearranging Ola's room, well the room on the other side of the house, and I looked out of the window and he was walking down the street, with his stick and his fedora and I know I'm not imagining it, I know he's real. When I tapped on the window he looked up at me and smiled and it was dad. But by the time I got to the front door the road was empty. I thought I was going mad. And if he is around what would I say to him? If I had the chance to talk to him I don't know if I'd have anything to say. Maybe he didn't die. Maybe he's haunting me. Or maybe I dreamed that I saw him. I don't know anymore.

When I came back from Nigeria the last time I dreamt a lot. But I didn't dream red dust on my floor, or feather's from white chickens appearing, or furniture moving, or fire appearing in the corner of my room. Ok, maybe I did dream the fire bit but nothing else. It all happened and my mum knew it was happening and she did things and it stopped. I pick up the phone.

'Dia, it's me. I don't feel well.'

'Come on, babe, what's up?'

'I can't go.'

'Beth, you woke me up on a Saturday morning to tell me this. Couldn't it wait? Are you making breakfast?'

'I'm not doing anything.'

She's put the phone down so now I have to get up. I open the curtains. I hate the garden in winter. Dad made a garden at the back of his compound. He planted all sorts of things that wouldn't grow. He had a greenhouse as well. I wonder if Ola has watered his plants. I suppose it doesn't matter now. I like having a brother. I suppose I could like having sisters if I knew them. If my dad had stayed here, I'm sure I would have had at least a sister. Although maybe not. It could have been a brother. Mum said that only girls were born in her family, but dad was from outside, so maybe it would have been different.

I don't know what to make for breakfast and Dia will be here soon.

'God, Kutes, you scared me, why are you creeping around the hallway?'

'I'm not creeping.'

'Aunty Dia's coming over. Are you getting the list from your nan?'

'No.'

'She isn't asking for much.'

'So why don't you do it then?'

She's obviously up to something, creeping around like that. I wouldn't have dared at her age. It was impossible anyway because my mum really did have ears in the walls. She didn't miss anything. She could be cooking, reading a book, and running a meeting all at the same time and she'd still know exactly what I was doing and where I was going. That's probably why she never had to ask who Kutes' dad was.

Kutes

she just doesnt get it ive got nothin to say to her an I wont have for the next however many years

it aint happenin bout 'you gonna get yer nans list' no im not you do it you do fuck all else so no I aint cos ive got me own shit to deal with sayin 'ooh anty dias comin' like thats gonna make a difference

itd be serves her right if I got off an went and lived with emre I swear not that im gonna but she goes on with herself an I just wanna no one simple thing an she cant hide behind that tear shit like she was abused or summat cos theres no way thered be a picture of me dad if she was so shes actin like shes a virgin or summat which is a bit of a laugh cos as far as I no virgins dont have babies unless there called mary an their kids called jesus and that aint me

anyways I aint wastin me time thinking bout her shit now ive got stuff to do

Ade

That day after James left, I went to my room. I wished to look through my clothes to decide what I would wear to work. I was seventeen, I wished to look fine. Two rough woollen skirts, two cardigans and two blouses with little rounded collars. There was little choice. I lifted my box from the corner and opened it. Taking out my wrappers one by one I tried to imagine what they would look like as skirts and blouses. My hand brushed against the package that I had forgotten about.

Opening the brown wax paper I cannot believe what I am seeing. Pounds. English pounds. I hold them in my hands and begin to cry. I cannot count it all for quite a while. When I do I find that there is one hundred pounds. My mind is fly-flying all around trying to work out where this has come from. My grandpapa had been a trader when he was younger. With wood and rubber. He traded with the British. Could it be from that? But, still, I do not know how it has arrived in my own luggage. Wrapping it again I put it back at the bottom of my box, underneath my wrappers. My breathing is coming fast and I am scared. I do not know why I am scared because I have not done anything wrong. Unable to settle I return to my box and open it once more. Removing each wrapper, a piece of paper falls out. It is from my old school notebook. The yellow lined paper is easy to recognise.

'Sista dis be for you to tek care o, my own mama does not miss it wen I tek some for years now. I beg o do not give it to him but keep it for you.'

Funmi. My own sweet Funmi has stolen from aunty, from her own mama. I do not feel bad. Aunty is a wicked woman. There were many times she went from the compound and did not return for days. The women made olofofo about these absences but Funmi always walked me away when they began their bad mind gossip, I kept quiet. Except I once asked Mama what Ashewo was and that was the last time I was allowed to go to the river. I do not know for sure how aunty collected so much English money but if Funmi has been taking it for many years it will not be missed. Opening the dresser drawer that holds my underwear I place the parcel at the back.

My sister, Funmi, was very wise when we were young. Although she did not know books and writing as well as myself, she knew of things that I did not. If it had not been for the money she gave to me I would not be living here now I am sure.

But my job-o! Heh! What a job that was. My hands became so sore in water all the time, washing-washing. So many glasses and cups and plates. It was a few weeks before I was allowed to give out food to the customers. There was one other girl my age who worked there. Sheila. She became my friend. Always it was a happy time in that restaurant. And the American soldiers, sha! They were very loud and laughed a lot. It was like a village party every night. And always talk of meetings and politics. I learned that in America most of those boys did not have a happy time and I was sad for them. There was one called Joe who would ask me out every time he saw me until Mr Konnen told him I had a young man, and then he changed his pleas to asking me to leave my young man and run away with him. But it was only in fun. Some nights, when James was not around, Olu would come and meet me to walk me home and if he could not Mr Konnen would arrange for somebody to walk with me. It was a very good job.

Many times when I was working I would listen to Mr Konnen talk about Pan-Africa. Back then, I did not know what this was. There would be students from different countries in Africa and they would ask him many, many questions about this Pan-Africa. He was a very good speaker, but I could not listen to it all as I was busy with my washing and chopping vegetables.

I spent many hours scrubbing pans and thinking about what I could do with my money. I wanted to go to school. I wanted to study.

Elizabeth

I can't cope with Kutes right now. She talks to me like I'm nothing, when she can be bothered talking. I can actually hear her laughing on her phone before she gets out of the house. She does it on purpose to show me that she's got a problem with me. God, it's cold in here, I'm sure I closed the living room window before I went to bed last night, but now I can see it's open. I can't go in.

'Morning chicken, not got the kettle on yet?'

'Dia, I closed the window last night and now it's open.'

'Well maybe you didn't put the latch on properly, it's no biggy. Come on I need coffee.'

But I did. I put the latch on properly because I always do. Dia's in the kitchen already making noise. Everything looks okay. The sofa's still pushed snug into the corner. I love that sofa. It's sexy. Which is a stupid thing to say about a sofa. But it's the way Dia said 'look at that Red. Leather. Sofa.' when we were shopping and the way she draped herself on it in the shop. But anyway it hasn't moved. Maybe I didn't close the window properly. Maybe.

'Are you coming in or are you just going to stand there while I make breakfast?'

I step over the threshold and close the door behind me. Dia is talking to me and I don't know what she's saying because there's something like a roar going on in my head and numbers are shouting out to be heard. I think my head might explode.

'Beth, sit down and drink this. What's happening?'

'Everything's so fucking loud.'

'Well of course it is. You're banging the brush on the window ledge, you can stop any time you like.'

And she's right. I didn't realise what I was doing. I look up at Dia and can see the concern in her eyes and I don't want to. I sit at the table opposite her. Dia always looks so fresh in the morning. Her extensions are sleek and smooth and her face glows. In fact, Dia hasn't changed since we were teenagers. I feel old and frumpy next to her.

'I don't think I'm feeling well.'

'Well that much is obvious.'

My dad has died, I've got to go to his funeral which means dealing with family I don't know and a place that makes me ill.

A big mouthful of coffee burns my tongue and the roof of my mouth.

'Beth, you can do it. You've just got to break it down. You know that.'

Her voice is so smooth and calm I almost believe her. When I feel like this I wonder why I'm not sharing my life with her properly. Why can't I just say, hey I'm gay and this is my girlfriend, deal. But I can't. I have to think about Kutes and my mum and my dad. Except that I don't have to think about my dad anymore because he's dead.

Dia's right. I just have to write a list. To break it all down. She's in the kitchen area again and I can smell waffles and she's put the radio on. I go over to the sideboard and take a pen and writing pad out of the left cupboard. Dia puts the waffles on the table and goes back for the syrup and brings more coffee.

'Right, waffle then write and let's get this sorted.'

And we sit at the table with weak sunlight coming through the windows and I can make believe that we're planning a holiday and that it's fun. When Dia leaves an hour later, I've got a list that I can work with and we've booked the plane tickets. We're flying with Air France at six thirty in the morning, change at Charles de Galle in Paris, and arrive in Lagos early evening. Breathe. Right, next. I have to phone the doctor's and arrange for Kutes and me to have our injections, but I'll have to check to see if my mum needs any. I don't know if you have injections if you're Nigerian or if you're immune already. Kutes won't be happy, she hates needles. And I have to get our visas. I don't know whether to do it by post or go down to London. I should have asked Dia. Maybe we can both go.

Kutes

Its like theres nothin that happens outside the house like she thinks the whole world is about her well its not an ive got other stuff to deal with

an it aint even like she asks me whats goin on just accuses me of stuff an it aint right dunno how me anty dia puts up with her

shes lucky I swear cos I could well go on at her about sneakin around but I love me anty dia an if I said summat shed probs stop her from comin round and then id have no one to talk to

she cant even work out that all shes gotta do is answer me proper wen I ask her things an she wont tell me nuthin I could scream its always about her dont even no why im wastin me time with this shit

anyways got stuff to do emres goin home to Cyprus for a bit and even tho I told him last week that I think we should have a break he still wants to see me today but carls is comin with me an then we can xmas shop an were goin out with everyone later so im not gonna let me mum put me on one

PARTY!

Ade

I cannot remember how long I was working in the restaurant, but it must have been for quite some time because I was cooking by then. I worked only on Saturday but this was enough for me. I had become very anxious at that time because I was not doing what I wanted to. James was not around very often and we did not spend any time alone. It was as though we had never been close. My own misery had not allowed me to worry about my mama at the beginning, but with so much time to think I began to feel sick with the thought of what I had done. I did not know how to write to mama and explain so I did nothing.

I spent time with Sheila on the days she was not working and when I was not in the house, cleaning. She would take me around Manchester. We came upon rubble that was once housing. I wondered why people had not come together and rebuilt their homes. This made Sheila laugh, 'we are not in a village now we are in Hingland!' She made me laugh the way she added letters to her words. But we did have some fun. Window shopping, even taking tea in hotel bars once or twice.

What a time that was. The house was becoming very full. Mainly men, so I did not get the chance to make new friends. I was now the one to write notes for the meetings. Mrs Kingsley had become very quiet and I knew that it was because her husband would not return. Almost one year had passed since he was reported missing. She had believed that he would return once the war was completed but it was not so. Life had become difficult for her.

Sometimes the men would speak so quickly I did not have time to write everything and o-oh those Jamaican accents when I first heard them. How so was that English? Their words ran into each other and rolled around the room. When two or three of those boys spoke at once it was as though they were singing with harmony. It did not take too long for me to relax my ear so that I could understand what they had to say, and truly, it was not so very different to my own people, it was just getting used to it. Independence was the most used word, and respect. At times I would feel my heart rise up in my chest until it seemed too large for my body. So many injustices. So many people suffering. How did we not know of this in our village?

Olu would walk out with me when he was in town. He attended meetings that were taking place all over the country. When he returned and came to me it was as though the air crackled around him, so much was his excitement.

'Ade, I tell you the day is coming!'

And he would swing me off my feet if we were in the park. Ah! This Olu. What a spectacle he would make. He had plans. To hear him speak you would imagine that one day he would rule the whole of Africa. For true!

James had been more and more absent. It was trade union meetings he told me when he returned, but Olu told me it was the communist party and that it was not a good thing. I did not tell James what Olu said but simply listened about what had happened in Cardiff and whom he had spoken to and how difficult life was for the coloured workers there. In my heart I had no interest in those politics. I intended to apply for school admission as soon as possible. Already the school year was about to commence and I had not secured a place. I had not told James that this is what I would do because I did not know how to tell him without showing him the money that Funmi had given to me.

There was also the problem that I was not receiving sponsorship from my village, although I had my school fees. I attended one college close to home and the woman sitting behind the desk could not even look at me. This woman with her red lips and chewing gum, she made me repeat myself again and again. Eventually the door behind her opened and an old man came through. He looked at me and smiled, kindly, I thought.

'Are you all right, dear?' he said to me. I was very grateful that he took the time to speak to me.

That painted woman said something about me wanting a job and how she could not understand me. She had to finish her letter, as though that was so important. I felt very foolish and my cheeks began to get hot. How could that silly woman believe I wanted to do some small job like she was doing?

I spoke very correctly. 'I have come to enquire about my application to study. I submitted it by hand one week ago.'

He called me dear again and waved his hand towards her. Then he was gone. And this woman, she told me that I was mistaken, that I would need to complete a further application for the next year as the courses were all full of English students. I simply turned and left. She did not know who I was. After that incident I found myself taking much more notice in the meetings. This colour bar that James told me of had become too real to me.

Elizabeth

I'm feeling better. We're all booked and we're going. I'll tell mum. I need to text Kutes. She won't reply, but I'm sure she'll turn up for dinner if I tell her Dia will be here. We can eat downstairs in Mum's room. It will be our first official meal since we moved back.

'Hiya, Mum, are you all right?'

'Close the door, Elizabeth, you are letting the heat out.'

God, she's on one, I don't know why I bother. She always brings me down.

'What are you doing?'

'I am arranging my papers. Will we not be travelling soon?'

'Yeah, but we're coming back. We're only going for a week.'

I'm not letting her do this. She can't wind me up. As if she's not coming back. Oh, god, what if she doesn't? What if something happens to her? She's so old and frail.

'You don't have to go, you know? I can do it. Really.'

'You cannot bury my husband, you can only bury your father.'

'What the hell does that mean? He's the same person.'

'Is this why you came to my room, to cause argument?'

She's done it again. Turned it all around as though it's me that's carrying on.

'I came to say Dia's coming over for dinner and I thought it would be nice if we all ate together. Kutes will be here too.'

'And I suppose it is myself who will be standing and cooking?'

'God, Mum, what's wrong with you? I'll cook. I'm trying to be nice.'

I wish I hadn't bothered coming down now. But she looks sad. Of course she's sad. And her hip. I keep forgetting.

'Mum have you taken any painkillers?'

'Yes-o I took them with breakfast. It is the cold, it gets into my bones.'

'Well, I've booked our tickets. For after Christmas. We're going on the thirteenth . I thought maybe we could talk about it, you know, with Kutes tonight.'

I'm not sure now about mum travelling. I keep forgetting that her hip needs replacing. She's so miserable. I'll do some shopping for her today. She can't need that much for Nigeria. She got her Christmas cards when I took her out last week. Maybe I should take her out more, but it's easier for me to just do it.

'Where's your list, mum? I'll go and get some of it this afternoon.'

'Is it not on the table?'

I haven't seen this album for years. My old school photographs. I'd forgotten about these old Polaroid's. They're so faded now. I must be about fifteen in that one. And there's Dia and me with our big Afros and black polo necks. We thought we were so cool. Well Dia was, she's even giving the black power salute. She took it all very serious. I wonder what happened to our consciousness. It's so easy when you're young and you can fight for things, but now, where's everything gone? I'm too tired to fight.

Maybe I'm not being fair. My job is a way of fighting. I'm trying to put things in place to make a difference for people. Who am I kidding? I listen to people. There's nothing to put in place. We make the right noises but it doesn't do anything, there's no funding to help anyone. I'm back in work on Monday. I'm going shopping.

'Do you need anything else, Mum? Any food?'

'No I have chicken, we will eat fried rice this evening.'

I forgot to ask about injections, but I can do it later. I can't wait to show Dia those photos. I wonder if Kutes will come back. She's not going to be happy but she won't say anything with Dia there though so it's a good time to tell her. I'm sure she's still seeing that guy. He's so old. But Dia says I can't mention it. Oh god, what if she gets pregnant to him. What if she's pregnant already? She could be. Maybe that's why she's so moody.

Kutes

Whos comin out later carls
Every1 its gonna be kickin
Is Wahida comin shes been a bit quiet has any1 seen her
shes bein sent back innit
Sent back where? She's more manc than you
Nah shes an asylum seeker or summat like that shes gotta go wen shes
18 I think
That's out of order she was in our school so shes been here for like eva
Yeah but its wot happens innit so wot time u comin over
Gotta have family dinna first but me anty diall be here so I can ask if
wahida can do anythin
Yeah good idea tho mebbe you should check first she might not want
you chattin her bizness
It aint like that weve gotta do things to help
Yeah ur rite kutes come down early an we can sort summat out b4 we
go wot u wearin?
That dress I got last week
Does emre no ur goin out lol
Haha yeah rite cos he can tell me what to do from cyprus innit
Wens he back then
Dunno dint ask him dont think im gonna see him wen hes back
anyways hes getting a bit clingy
Gud
Wot do yer mean gud theres nothin wrong with him
I dint mean that jeez chill out I just mean we can go out more innit
Anyways Im gonna get some stuff done before dinna Ill text u wen Im
leaving yeah

Ade

Was it not like old times this evening? True we were all women but that did not make any difference. This friend of Elizabeth's speaks like a man. She has no fear to put forward what she is thinking. Has she not always been a good influence? And now my granddaughter listens to her when she cannot hear anyone else. This is good. In this country girls are educated in these ways. It was not so for me. I had to listen well and learn what was happening whilst cooking.

At the cafe it was becoming very excitable. So many people were coming and going. Talking, always talking. Across tables, across the room, even while there was a band playing. It was as though I could catch the atmosphere and ride it around the world, to Africa, to America and the West Indies. Oh-o! So much talk of rights; workers rights, Negro's rights, coloured's rights. Everybody had rights and I must confess that I, too, believed I had rights. But of course I did not enter into any of the discussions, I simply cooked yam and cassava and chicken and meat, when it was available.

I listened and I planned in my head what I would do in my own village when I returned. I decided that I would be a lawyer. I would make contracts and know how to address judges and make sure that all my clients were given what was their own by right. Yes, I was going to be so clever and respected. Perhaps I would organise people together to make our village renowned, and all of Nigeria would pass by to see how this had happened, and the strangers would want me to come to their own village and show them how to do these wonderful things. I could not specify what these wonderful things would be. This is what the money in my underwear drawer had done to me. I thought I could own the world.

I had not yet received any letter from Funmi and I was too scared to write to her. I did not know if she would still be in Papa's house. Not once did I think about how my mama would be feeling not to hear from me in two months. I was ashamed. I did not know what to say to her. I was waiting until I was married to James so that I could tell her, but James was away so much we had not spoken about it.

Mr Konnen had not been in the restaurant when I arrived one Saturday, but he came later, before closing. He had been travelling to other cities. Oh, so much excitement. He stood on the steps of the restaurant with the door closed behind him. With the smoke circling him he looked like a water god rising from the river. Slowly, all the talking stopped and I felt my own heart slow down while he stood as though surveying his village. When he began to talk nobody moved. It was as though the world had stopped and Mr Konnen was in another time. A conference. Right here in Manchester, he said. Across the road at the town hall. Heh! The room erupted like a sudden burst of rain at the beginning of rainy season. The cheers bounced around, hitting the floor and the walls and leaving their mark. The men jumped up and hugged each other, pushing forward to go up and pat him on the back or hug him hard.

Suddenly a bottle of London's Gin appeared. It was only very occasionally that a bottle of something strong was seen. I think it was kept for special occasions. First a libation was poured for our ancestors. Each African man called a name and intoned his own prayer. It lasted long long. It also reminded me of being in Papa's yard at his meetings and I felt some loss. But when the libations were finished everyone began to talk at once. Big groups, small groups, twos and threes. Chatting, chatting and drinking from gin, whisky and beer. It was as though there was no ration and the war had not finished just a few months before.

The music started at some point while Sheila and I were busy serving food, washing plates, watching and listening. The gramophone in the corner was busy with Louis Armstrong and Nat King Cole, they even played women like Ella Fitzgerald and Billie Holiday and I felt my foot start to tap. At some tables the voices became louder to be heard over the music, at others they sang along to the records. What a time we had o! My chest swelled with the happiness that was in that room. Sheila and I grinned at each other and snapped our fingers to the beat.

It was difficult not to be affected by so much excitement, at some point Sheila and I laughed and danced around our kitchen area. It did not take too long for the men to begin dancing. With so few women in the restaurant Sheila and I were their targets. They did not even give us time to remove our aprons before they took our arms and glided in between the tables with us. We would dance with one and then another would be waiting to take his place. It was so much fun and the men would pretend to argue about whose turn it was next. In between records we would have to sneak away to the kitchen to find some food or drink for someone or just to breathe and fan our faces. I did not know what a Pan African Conference was, but it was going to be a good thing.

Yes, the celebrations lasted long into the night and much food and drink was taken. I became quite exhausted and I am sure the day was breaking by the time I began to walk home with Olu.

Elizabeth

Kutes is getting involved in something that's political. Obviously she doesn't think about it like that, it's just her friend that she's helping out. But it is political. The same kinds of things are out there right now that were around all those years ago when we were fighting.

That makes me sound political too, and we were. There was so much going on. I really believed that I simply went to meetings with Dia at first, then for Femi later, but actually when we were talking about it earlier I realised that it was real. We believed in something and we did stuff and we expected changes to take place. Just like Mum I suppose, except she did see some real changes. Didn't all those people she knew go back to Africa and run countries or something? While here we just got the suss law and riots and hard times.

I must be in a bad mood, because it wasn't like that. We were warriors with big hair and organisations. Dia and I were always going down to London for different demonstrations. Angela Davis. There was a big march for her. We'd catch the train or someone would be driving in the old Cortina and we'd all pile in the back. We had such a laugh those days wondering if we were going to make it, seeing how many of us could fit in. God, that car stank. It was a wonder we survived it. Stale cigarettes and petrol is how I remember it. Squashed up beside Dia with Jen and at least two more in the back and a couple in the front. It was someone's dad's car and it always had to be back before his shift at 6:00 am on the Monday morning. We'd take it in turns to stay awake and talk to whoever was driving to make sure we didn't end up on the other side of the motorway. God, we must have been crazy. I'd kill Kutes if I thought she was doing that. But there were so many women's groups. We had things in Manchester but Dia liked to go and join the big rallies. We got involved in all sorts of fights that weren't really about us but they were about women. Women's rights in factories, to control their own bodies, to work where they wanted, get a good education for their children. We were out there and we were doing stuff and it was natural and normal and we couldn't have been any other way. To have hundreds of women standing together who could shout and demand and be strong. We loved being a part of it all.

And now Kutes is taking up a cause and I feel frightened because it's different these days, especially if her friend is a Muslim. Now it's all about religion and I don't want her to write anything on the net that could affect her getting into university or getting a good job. Oh, god, if Dia heard my thoughts she'd go mad. And she'd be right to. It doesn't matter what religion her friend is because rights are rights.

My dad was a communist sympathiser if I think about it. And he was all right. The Cold War had its witch-hunts so it was no different from today. Mum would hit him with his socialist newspaper when it was delivered. She didn't want it bringing interest to our house.

I was excited when Dad was around. He was new. I could hardly remember him because he'd been away for so long. I remember him coming back. He didn't stay in our rooms downstairs, but he was always around. He took me on his protests for Biafra. There was an office in Didsbury. We had placards and it was my job to stick paper on the cardboard so that people could write on it. There were marching songs too, but I didn't know the words, they weren't in English.

Once, Dad was talking to someone over by the stage. I was supposed to be sticking the paper on cardboard, but the glue was all over my fingers and I couldn't stand it. I slipped away from the table and looked around for a sink. Tucked away behind the old upright piano, I found a cracked, dirty sink. There were cups stacked on a wooden shelf next to it. I just had to reach the tap and I could get the glue off my fingers. I dragged the piano stool around and climbed on it. Turning the tap on and rubbing my hands together I tried to dislodge the glue. A face appeared beside me with eyes so wide and skin so dark and shiny I almost screamed.

'We know your daddy is a spy. Is the white man who keeps this war going. Is your daddy-o.'

I didn't dare breathe. She began laughing and I was ready to start crying.

'Aunty, come now. You will fear the child, making noise like this.' And one of the ladies from the sticking table led away the old, bent over woman to a chair. There was nothing scary about her. She was just an old lady. I'd forgotten about that.

Mum didn't come to those marches and I didn't understand why. Obviously I didn't understand what was going on either. It was later, at the end, when those awful pictures were being shown on television. There was a teacher, Miss Brown, who insisted on calling me a little Biafran when we did dance drama. Mum went to the school and gave her a good talking to. We're Nigerians, she said, not Biafrans, and the teacher didn't know the difference.

Kutes

So I tells me aunty dia that wahida is bein sent back an its like im sat in the bloody citizens advice cos me mum an me nan are like chippin in an givin advice an stuff and it aint like its their job like me aunty dia deals with this innit cos shes a social worker with kids an I know wahida aint really a kid but that's how were classed cos we aint eighteen yet

so me nans like yeah it was like this back in the day when I arrived an they dint want us an im like us who yeah cos im born an bred but shes goin on about colonialism an shit which is like slavery days innit an then she says we need to do meetings and shit an like what does she think weve been doin an its my job to find out stuff duh

then me mums goin on about black power an stuff an her an me aunty dia starts reminiscin bout angela davey or someone an wearin black berets like french dudes an telling me we need to do protests and rallys whatever they are an its like they think we dont know nothin dint hear me mum sayin protest when we went an did proper big things in town bout the iraq war innit fact I can only remember her goin on about gettin arrested an missin exams an trouble startin

finally me aunty dia takes me serious an tells me about some organisations an the things we can do cos at college were gonna do a proper protest an were puttin on a dance to raise some money an theres bands an stuff who are playin for free an someones gettin in touch with the metro paper cos it aint right she dint ask to come here she was sent an it aint fair that after all this time they should try an send her back its out of order

Ade

Ah! What a time we had in that one-week. So many people arrived to take part in our conference and many of them stayed in our house. I have the records somewhere because Mrs Kingsley kept a meticulous guest book. I must look for it. It was so exciting for a young girl to take part in. On the Sunday evening before it all began Mr Konnen asked for me to work. And what work that was. So many men all talking, talking, and the food-o. I do not know where Mr Konnen found all the meat that we prepared and I do not know how it was all eaten so quickly. Every second Sheila and I were passing food to the girls who were serving. And the dirty plates-o. I was sure the skin would leave my hands I did so much washing.

Olu was there of course, and James, although I do not recall any other white men but I am sure there must have been some. At times the noise rose so high I thought that there would be some fighting but always Mr Konnen's calm voice was heard over everything else and laughter would take the place of anger. We were all on the same side, that's what he said, and it was true. All these men had come together and they were on the same side. There were students and lawyers and doctors from everywhere in the world: Nigeria, the Gold Coast, Sierra Leone, Nyasaland, Gambia, South Africa and then from America and Trinidad and Jamaica and other islands and I do recall that there were some Indian men. What a night we had.

Sheila told me how things were in Jamaica. Her sister had written about the men in their town who had not returned from the war and those who had returned with ideas that they were now British and should be treated like the white man. Sheila's sister said the girls were fighting for these men who knew 'foreign' but the men who returned only wanted their girlfriends who they had left or been writing to. Sheila said there would be trouble-o. We laughed about this while we cooked, served and washed plates. They are coming, we said. Those men are coming. You cannot fight for your country and not come.

The restaurant had been quiet the week before because Mr Konnen and others had been in Paris. Of course, Sheila and I could only imagine what that was like to be in Paris. We had heard on the radio about the fashion, the couture that was coming back, and we spent time discussing the hats that we would buy if we were there. Of course, the men did not have time to be looking at hats, the discussions that took place when they returned were serious. Trade union business. Freedom for coloured workers. The Labour Party, the party for the people. And of course, we listened to that too, but we were young. We wanted hats. But we were so busy we did not spend time that night talking about fashion.

When we moved on to dancing later in the evening we were so happy to be there. All evening, cooking, washing up, clearing tables, cleaning floors, emptying ashtrays. Eh-eh! Non-stop, o! My apron itself looked as though a party had happened on it. Gravy, beer, grease, tomato stains. The whole evening was presented down the front of me. It took so long to get it clean, even Mrs. K's box of Oxydol was not enough. But when the dancing started, I did not even think about that apron. Sheila and I looked at each other and grinned. We threw those dirty things off, smoothed down our dresses, took turns at the little sink in the corner with the cracked mirror and made ourselves look presentable. Sheila brought out a bottle of 4711 cologne that she kept for emergencies and we were soon ready to go.

I remember one man was very slick on the dance floor and we all watched him when he began making his moves. I cannot remember who that was now. But he twisted and shimmied and we all tried to dance up close to him, even the other men. He was doing some version of the shuffle and I knew that. Funmi and I had practiced well-well when we were young. Swinging our hips and side stepping here and there. Even with my little heels on I could still throw some moves and shapes and soon people were watching me, too. Sheila whistled through her fingers like a common worker, but that man-o he sidled up to me and began to match his moves to mine. Hei, we danced. Sweat was coming down his face like rain down the window but he did not stop, just loosened his jacket and gripped my waist. We were back in the village, soft red earth under our feet, parents not taking enough notice to stop us. We gyrated and grinned and shuffled and laughed. Soon others joined in and the smell of his cologne and brylcreem and fresh sweat mingled with everybody else's. He bowed low and kissed my hand as the music changed beat and I had to go and sit down to catch my breath.

Next it was Sheila's turn to dance with him as the music changed rhythm to a more ragtime style. I couldn't take my eyes off him and it was a while before I realised that James was scowling at me from the next table. That man with his miserable face. I turned back to the dancing and watched Sheila and that magic dancer match step for step. Even though he was not a particularly small man, beside her he looked it and it was hard to see who was swinging who. But his footwork was something to see. Even now I can remember the gasps of the other men when he did something fancy, those black and white brogues seeming to be carried along on wheels. The spins, false trips, full stops. What a dancer. He made it look effortless. His friends began to nudge him as though to make him lose his rhythm. He grinned. This was a man who loved to move and who loved to be watched because he knew he was good. What was his name, now? Sheila came over and dragged me back to the floor and we danced for at least one more hour. Even Olu came and danced with us at one point, though his moves were not as smooth as that man. What is happening that I can forget a name so easily? Am I old now? It was not Padmore, he was very serious and did not dance. He liked to smoke and drink and talk-talk. And I would have known if it was Jomo because that hat did not move from his head and he could not have danced with that on.

Ah, Nkrumah, that's who it was. I have a picture of him somewhere. Not dancing. He was here in this kitchen. At a meeting. Someone came with a box brownie and took a picture. It was funny how everyone around the table stopped in mid sentence when the picture was being taken and looked as though they were already imprinted, myself included. I believe that was taken during the week of the conference. Hei, Kwame Nkrumah. I had forgotten that he was here. But they were all here and they were all students and nobody knew that they would become big men.

At the end of the evening, when the dancing finished, groups left together to find their lodgings. James had left with one group to direct them and I walked home with Olu and three or four other men who were staying in our rooms. Olu tucked my arm firmly into his and talked about politics with the men until we reached the front door. From what I could tell they were simply repeating what had been said in the restaurant all evening, but the excitement that they had was catching. I could hardly sleep that night. I was sure that the next day would make so many changes in our lives and I sat down on the chair by my window with a blanket around my shoulders and wrote a letter to Funmi. It was time. I wanted to tell her about everything. How I wished she had been there with me to share all of this.

The next morning I woke early so that I could help Mrs Kingsley with preparing the porridge. It was good to see her cheerful. We stirred the pans and she told me she was going to live with her sister after Christmas.

I asked after her sister and where she lived. It was St. Anne's, next to the sea with good air to breathe, she told me. I asked about the house and she said she would sell it. This did not please me.

The atmosphere around the table that morning dispelled my bad mood, so much enthusiasm for the day ahead. Planning, planning and talking about what would be. We all walked together to the town hall, even Mrs Kingsley came along. It was a cold morning but the sky was blue with a false sun. In the park, squirrels were scratching in the fallen leaves, such pretty red colours blending in with their surroundings, not like the grey ones we have today. Two of the students who were with us had only arrived in the country at the same time as me and they started crunching through the dry leaves and kicking them in the air.

Elizabeth

We've had such a good time tonight. Dia looks so chilled. I'll show her that photo album and we'll listen to Dexter Gordon.

'Dee, I'm not sure about Kutes getting involved in this stuff.'

'What stuff, Elizabeth?'

I don't know what's wrong with me. Words jump out of my mouth when I'm not paying attention.

'She's got A' levels coming up. She's seeing a guy old enough to be her grandad. And she won't even speak to me.'

'Right, so because she's being a teenager, she shouldn't support her friend who may be deported and it would be a really bad thing for her to think about something outside of herself? Is that what you're saying?'

'You missed out the bit about her seeing Emir.'

'His names Emre and I've told you it won't last long. Anyway he's gone back to Cyprus. She won't be seeing him again.'

'How do you know that?'

'Does it matter who she tells as long as you know?'

Breathe. She's right. Of course she's right. But Kutes is my daughter. She should be telling me those things.

'And Beth, don't you think it's about time you told her about her dad?'

'We're not on that subject.'

So Kutes has managed to ruin my night. Great. Thanks. She doesn't need to know who her dad is because he isn't around. He went off and married his fiancée, had 2.4 children and lived happily ever after in London. He didn't really get in touch with me after he left, so why would I look for him.

'Anyone would think you still have feelings for him, Beth. If he'd stayed around we wouldn't be together, would we? Or perhaps that doesn't matter.'

'Why are you going on like this? I'm with you. I've always been with you. You know that. If it wasn't for Femi we wouldn't have Kutes. Have you thought about that? I'd been ill. He was nice. He made me feel safe.'

'And he was handsome and so much fun and you just couldn't keep your eyes or your hands off him, could you? I was the one who was around when you were ill. I didn't see him doing much.'

I want to lie on the floor and scream. I can't believe this is happening now. Is it too much to ask that we have a nice night? Now I can't breathe, my chest is collapsing in on itself.

'Come here, Beth. I'm sorry. Don't be upset. I'm sorry. Take deep breaths. Have you got a paper bag? Come on, hon.'

Why doesn't she know how much I love her? Femi has nothing to do with it. It's just that he didn't stay in touch. He doesn't know Kutes. And she didn't need him. Dia's always been here. She should understand that.

'I don't want to argue.'

'Relax, I'll open some more wine.'

Kutes

Im proper worried about wahida cos it dunt look as though anythin weve done so far is gonna make a difference an she said that theres people who used to live in her building yeah an they would go an sign on not like the dole but at a place where asylum seekers have to go an then they just like disappeared

but wahida dunt have to do that cos shes got a social worker an stuff an that agency got her a proper solicitor an theyre writin to mps an everythin it aint fair that some peeps have gotta go through all that shit what difference does it make if one persons here yeah cos shes been here for years an it aint like its a drain on society

it aint right people should just be able to go where they want innit like me grandad he was in Nigeria an he werent born there so why shud he be allowed to live where he wants an other peeps cant its out of order like everyone wants to come here an live in a shitty little flat yeah

an ive seen pics at me nans an aunty lives in a proper big house with marble floors an she looks well better off than us an me nan says she dint go school an that she taught her to read an write so if peeps can work hard an get all that its better somewhere else than here innit cos if you dont go school here ya aint getting nowhere its well messed up

but dunno why im getting so deep when its not bout us is it its about wahida an anyways well make sure she has a good time tonight an the metro reporter says hes gonna cover it so therell be a story in the paper so that should do summat

but shell have to look sad in the pics not like shes enjoyin it so ill have to tell her that then when theyve gone we can proper party an if she aint goin anywhere for xmas dinner ill tell her to come to ours

Ade

So Elizabeth has travelled to London. So many times she would go there
when she was younger, to fight the cause. Did she not know that there
was cause in Manchester? They played at politics. Wearing black uniforms
and shouting slogans. It was not like that in my day. We were organised.
Did we not put on the best conference?

What an atmosphere, sha! So many people around the door chattering
and punching each other in the arm. Oh, and the accents fighting each
other and flying around heads like birds circling the trees. It promises to
be a very good day. I find Sheila in the crowd, standing to one side. We
lower our hats so that we can look at all the men without being seen.

'What of that one, Sheila, is he not a prince?'

'Ade, wha' you go look pon cloth an tink prince. Da man jus' scrub up
well.'

'Sheila you are bad, these men are important-o.'

We giggle and nudge each other when one pretty man goes past,
guessing which country he comes from and whether he is important.
James signals for me and pushes us through the crowd and we go inside.

I had never been inside a building like that one. Of course, I had only
been in this country less than three months. The ceilings were high-high
and the hall was like an inside compound. James brought me to the front
bench and I did not think that we should sit there, I was sure that many
important people would take that place. I waited for one of the officials
to ask us to move, a white man with a black woman sitting right at the
front, but nobody came. James watched people come in, said hello to
some, stood up and shook other's hands. I thought he would bow when
that terrible Charles man came in but he did not. Sheila winked at me as
she went past and I wished I could sit with her near the back.

Once people are seated James turns to me, 'this is it, Ade, we'll be going
home soon, you'll see, you wait and see.' And I cannot respond to him
because the meeting begins but I have no intention of returning home
until I have completed my studies. I have not even written to Mama,
she does not know what has happened to me. How then can I think of
returning? I want to say these things to James but he has turned his head
and is looking up at the stage. It is as though he does not remember why
we travelled. My belly should be round and full now and I should be
his wife. But neither of these things are happening. How can I think of

returning home to look Mama in the face?

So that first morning there were two worries in my head about where I would live when Mrs Kingsley sold her house and the fact that I had not yet begun to study and yet James was talking of taking me home. I studied the flags of African countries that were around the walls. Many of them I recognised from my school studies. There were so many posters behind the platform that we had prepared the day before. 'Freedom for all subject peoples' 'Down with the Colour Bar' 'Africa for the Africans' 'Africa Arise'. Sheila and I had helped with them and I wanted to add some illustrations but one man told me it would detract from the message. I liked how they looked at the front of the hall.

I counted the people on the platform, there were seven and I was very surprised to see that there were two women up there. I had missed the introductions so I did not know the names but I could not take my eyes off the women. So after all this was not a conference for men to decide things, this was for everybody. It was easier to listen than to think about my own problems. I did not like the uncomfortable feeling that I carried inside.

The stories began about right here in England and I must confess I was surprised. I did not expect that to happen. So many children being abandoned in this country if their father was a coloured man. In some places they were even trying to make them leave the country and go to their father's land. How could this be so, when most of the fathers had gone back to sea and did not know of the children? I had in my mind a picture of babies being placed in great carriers and taken out to sea with no mother to feed them and sing to them and tell them stories. I began to dream how I would be a lawyer of the children. I would take on their case. It was only James moving around and tapping his foot that brought me back into the great hall and the reality that perhaps I would not be staying long enough to study.

Every time a speaker stopped there was great applause, even from James who I knew was feeling very impatient. He wanted to hear about Africa and had little interest in what was happening in Cardiff and Liverpool. However, I understood and so should he about the protocol for meetings, had he not been to many with my papa who always began with libation to our ancestors. Meetings should always begin with what is closer to home and in this case home was right here in England.

I did not listen closely to all that was being said because I had so many worries to deal with. It was not until the afternoon when one of the women, she was Jamaican, spoke for a short while. This woman was clever, sha! Amy Garvey. She spoke eloquently and everybody listened carefully. She told us about the black woman. Well she said Negro but that is not a word that we use today. She said how we were pushed into making babies and not taken seriously. It was the poor women who were the most political; and teachers, women teachers were the most active. This made me think that perhaps I should be a teacher and not a lawyer. I wanted to be like this woman and only if I was able to study would I be there. I had not seen Olu for most of the day, he had been with other students so I could not discuss with him but I had to make my plans so that when the conference was over I would know what I had to do. O, how I missed my sister Funmi.

After the last debate, Mrs Kingsley came to me and said we must hurry home. We had to prepare an evening meal for our guests. I advised James and we left quickly. Mrs Kingsley was in a very spirited mood and she talked to me about how her sister lived in a large house and Mrs Kingsley wanted to make it into a place that could house coloured children. The speakers had made her feel terribly guilty that she had not done enough although I pointed out to her that many students from Africa and the West Indies would not have had anywhere to stay if she had not opened her home and offered them rooms. She did not appear to hear me. She would need one hundred pounds to start and she must sell her house quickly. My heart dropped because that would mean I would have nowhere to live.

I fell into my bed exhausted that first night and I am sure every night after that during the conference. There was so much work to do and still I went to the conference every day.

I did not sit with James after the second day but with women who were determined that they also had contributions to make to our new Africa. We listened to many stories of how the colonies, our very own countries, were being treated and I realised that this is what my own papa and Uncle Tunde had been involved in. Those small meetings in our compound had been about this union activity. And my papa disappearing to meetings around the country had been a direct result of this activity. I became frightened. Had Papa not been gone for two weeks before I left? Had Mama not been very sad? I felt ashamed. I did not know how to write to Mama and explain myself, but I knew I must.

Elizabeth

We've left it late to get the visas. Mum gave me the name of someone who works there, in the visa office. He'll sort it out quick-quick she said.

'Beth, can't you relax for one second?'

'What do you mean?'

'If you grip the cup any tighter you'll crush it.'

'What will Kutes get up to while I'm gone? I should have brought her.'

'Oh for god's sake Beth. Kutes is seventeen. And let's face it you hardly see her anyway. Which is about right for that age.'

'But what if she gets arrested or something?'

'Read this. It's about an exhibition. And Beth...'

'Yes?'

'I know you're planning and scheming, but forget it. We're on a break and not on a military operation. Just chill out.'

She opens one eye and we grin at each other.

She always knows. It was the same when we went out for the night when we were younger. We'd start the evening so crisp in our glittery waistcoats and platform boots. Even Dia would take off her black polo neck and black power face for a Saturday night out. The evening would end with smudged blue eyeliner, glitter eyeshadow on our cheeks, no lipstick and cockeyed afros. We danced, we sang, we knew every lyric to every song and every shoulder shrug and foot shuffle.

There was one night when I let Dia talk me out of organising us. It wasn't like I did much anyway, I just arranged with our other friends and made sure someone was driving our way to drop us off and that they were driving back our way to drop us home. Just normal stuff. But for some reason that night I relaxed. She'd been going on before we left for the Reno and she probably convinced me to have a drag on her spliff, or gave me a blow back more like, I can't remember. But I do remember she was lecturing me about relaxing more and going with the flow or something like that.

We drank too much, far too much, but it was such a good night. Dancing in the dark, screaming songs down each other's ears, grinding up in the corner with random guys. And then there was a police raid. It hadn't happened for a long time so it was a surprise. Dia grabbed my arm and dragged me out through the crowds. We couldn't find anyone we knew to take us home so we ended up in a taxi. By the time we got back neither of us had platforms on and the taxi driver was cussing us for our singing. Gloria Gaynor, I will Survive, non-stop, with actions. It was Dia's way of chilling me out. I was trying to be polite and not laugh out loud and we were leaning into each other. She smelled good. Cigarettes, rum and a faint whiff of Yves Saint Lauren.

The trick was to get into the house without waking mum up. We'd made it to the first floor landing when her door opened. We froze. Hands over our mouths trying to stop giggles slipping out. The bathroom door creaked open and we let out our breaths. I wanted to get up to my room quick, but Dia sneaked down a few stairs and stuck her head through the bannister. I dragged her away; we still had to get past the tenant's rooms without being seen. It's not like I wasn't allowed out, but these guys treated me like a little sister and were up in my business, I didn't need another lecture about drinking.

When we got upstairs we played the radio quietly while Dia smoked the rest of her spliff out of the window, she said she'd seen a guy's arse in the bathroom and she reckoned it was Olu because it definitely wasn't my dads. I didn't want to know. We got into bed back to back with our feet touching, we slept like that then. The room spinning, ears ringing and my best friend at my back.

Pushing further into my seat I take a deep breath.

Kutes

Me mum thinks ive forgotten bout me dad but I aint just cos Ive been busy I told me anty dia that I was gonna say summat but she was like well shall we leave it for a bit an im like we! cos its about me innit there aint no we

an I understand that im lucky yeah cos like wahida aint got anyone at all cept us lot an if she gets sent back she wont even have us and it does make yer think about things but still it aint like were in the 50s or summat there aint no reason for secrets an hiding an shit its the effin 21st centry now innit things are different anyways I wont say anything before xmas cos it would spoil it for me nan and that aint fair cos shes old innit

oh shit wots emre ringin me for now I told him I aint seein him any more I aint answerin it

Ade

Soon it will be time for us to travel. It has been difficult to remember. Is this not why we keep photographs and letters? The week that I spent amongst all of these people at the conference made an impact on what happened next for me. I did not know, as I sat there listening to stories of America and South Africa and the Caribbean islands and all the African countries in between, that I would become involved in politics. On the final day, the two women were the first speakers, Amy Garvey and Alma La Badie. I remember their names well-well because only they spoke up there with all the men. They were so very passionate about what was happening in their island and it put me in mind of my own village. I had not experienced this second-class woman phenomenon because in my family only women were born and we were educated and treated well. In fact, my mama was highly educated and respected in our village so for myself I did not understand that there were classes of women. It was when I had chance to speak to Olu, in the evening as we dined, that it became clear to me and I was ashamed.

Of course my mama, our family, were of the rich class, and all that I took for granted was not available for other women in our village. I took my mind to some of the walks I would take with Funmi, and I could picture the squat houses by the river that looked as though they would not stand through a rainy season. I remembered women who each year would walk with pregnancy apparent, all the time looking older and more ragged. I vowed that I would help my village. Once James and I were married and I had a certificate and maybe a baby we would return. And that was my resolve and my intention. Yet somehow, once the conference was over, and all the great speakers had gone, and the students returned to their cities, I had more immediate concerns. My intentions were pushed to the back of my mind.

Mrs Kingsley received a letter from her sister. I walked into the kitchen and caught her mood immediately. She was flap-flapping her hands, pacing the floor. It was as though she was a bird trapped in a small space and did not know what to do. This was what she had been waiting for. The last of her sister's lodgers had left her home and now it was time for her to pack up and begin a new life in St. Anne's. I had strong doubts about her project. My main concern, however, was not about these children and Mrs Kingsley, but about where I would live. I had not had the opportunity to speak to James during the conference and once it was over he had been travelling around the country attending other meetings. Olu had commenced studying once more and had returned to London and the few acquaintances I made had now left the house and only two or three male students remained. I had to make my own decision.

In my box, hidden in my wrappers, I had £110. Each week I had placed a little change to Funmi's money. I had to decide what would happen about my studies if I chose to give this amount to Mrs Kingsley and took possession of her house. I knew that I would be sacrificing my studies. I could pay my own schooling, I had enough, and I could find somewhere else to live, and I would still have enough to return home when I was ready. But somehow, it was this house. I had a very strong feeling and had become attached and I justified that many black students would have difficulties finding somewhere to reside if Mrs Kingsley's house was not available.

I spent several sleepless nights working out my plans and changing my mind. I had nobody to discuss this with and it made me quite ill, as though I had eaten bad meat. But the decision was taken out of my hands once a gentleman visited the house to make a viewing. There were two students and myself in the kitchen when he arrived. He had a look of horror on his face when he saw us and asked Mrs Kingsley outright if this was the kind of company she kept. He told her that obviously the price she was asking of £150 was quite unreasonable because it was a house of ill repute and would take quite some time to remove the taint. What a rude man! Mrs Kingsley went very still and as the man stood there so smug in his whiteness and his thoughts that he had got one over on a woman, she began to give him a lashing with her tongue that reduced him to a small boy. Hah! What a thing.

'Excuse me. Who do you think you are? You low life good for nothing. You think I can't hear your southern la-de-da accent? And you dare to come in here and talk about my doctors and lawyers like that. You should be ashamed of yourself. It's the likes of you that's a problem here. Getting above your station, thinking you can diddle a woman like this. Get away with you.'

We watched with our mouths open as she went red in the face with the effort of telling this man about himself. Her hair that was always pulled so neatly into a bun at the back of her head seemed to spring out to join in the affray. Although small and skinny, at that moment I am sure she grew ten inches and widened her girth. Needless to say she did not sell it to him.

We cheered her as the man left but she sat down and cried. She did not know what to do. Because of the war that had only finished that year, people did not have money to throw around on houses that needed to be modernised and updated. The two male students left the room, in embarrassment I am sure, and I comforted her as best I could. Once she had calmed and I had made her a cup of tea I told her of what I had been thinking. I offered her £100 and I requested that she accept this in exchange for the house and we would draw up a contract where I would pay her the remaining balance over the following years. What I had not done was to make sure that I was allowed to own property but I did not think this would be a problem, it felt as though it was meant to happen. The next weekend Olu came to visit and we discussed this matter with him because he was studying law. Once it was agreed that we could go ahead, it once more brought tears to her eyes and she stood and hugged me for a long time. So that was it. At eighteen years old I became the owner of a large house and a landlady. My plans had changed rapidly.

When James returned to Manchester, he was not impressed.

'What do you mean you've bought a bloody house, Ade?'

'I have not bought a house, James, I have purchased this house.'

'Don't you think it's something you should have discussed with me first?'

'Were you here for me to discuss with you, James?'

He is pacing around my room and trying not to raise his voice too loud. He knows the students will come to see what is happening, because I am their small sister.

'Ade, where did you get that kind of money? Don't you think we could have used it for other things?'

'It was my money. Do I ask you for anything? In fact I have not asked you for one kobo since we arrived here and you have not offered me anything.'

'You think you can live here for free, Ade? Has Mrs K ever asked you for a penny?'

I had not considered this fact and felt ashamed. I believed that helping to clean and keep house was enough.

'See, Ade, there's things you don't think about. Now let's stop this nonsense. You know we're going back soon. There's nothing here for us, so tell Mrs K you've changed your mind.'

But of course I cannot because I have signed the contract and given the money to her. Rather than tell him this I cry. That evening James placed another baby in my womb.

Elizabeth

I've bought a Christmas tree and I don't know where to put it. I wanted Kutes to come and help but she isn't talking to me. When I was young we always had a small tinsel tree on the sideboard at the back of the room, you wouldn't even notice it if you didn't know it was there. But we did have parties. Lots of them. There were always people knocking on the door and bringing food and laughing and talking loudly.

'Mum, I've got a tree, where shall I put it?'

'What a size is this, daughter? Do you think we live in a great hall-o?'

'It's not that big I just thought it would be nice. We could decorate it tonight, all of us.'

She points to the corner at the back of the room by the sideboard and I drag it over there. I don't know why I'm doing this. Kutes will be going out and my mum has no interest in a tree. But Dia will be here. She'll get into the spirit of things. I leave the netting on and take a brush out to clear the pine needles in the hall. I left the front door slightly ajar when I came in and I can see a shadow through the crack in the door.

'Hello, who's there?'

I switch on the light and walk towards the door keeping an eye out for any movement upstairs. Holding my breath, I pull the door open quickly. There's nobody there.

When I go back into my mum's she's got more photographs out on the table. There's one of me that I'd forgotten about. I'm around six years old and I'm sitting on my dad's knee at this table. There's a large Christmas tree behind us in the same place that I've put this one. It's bare and lopsided. Our normal tinsel one is in its usual place. I don't ever remember my dad being home at Christmas. There's a present standing on the floor next to us and I'm smiling a big gap-tooth smile. I have on a terrible stiff looking dress and I can't tell what colour it is, it's just a lighter shade of grey. My dad is looking to the side and seems to be talking to someone who's off camera. He's got a tight fitting suit on and a fedora on the side of his head. I look at my mum to ask her about it but she's sifting through papers and photographs and muttering to herself.

I pick up a few more of the small, square black and white photos. There's another one of me with my dad but this time Mum has come into the photograph and Dad's looking straight at the camera. He has a big smile on his face and I'm stood to one side of him now, the present is just

129

visible in the corner. He has one arm around my shoulders and the other around my mum's waist, she's not smiling. I'm looking at the present.

'Mum when was this? I don't remember it. Why can't I remember?'

'What do you mean you cannot remember? It is there in front of you, is it not?'

'I mean I really don't remember it being taken.'

She takes the photograph from me and looks at it closely.

'You do not remember the orange dress you wore? Like a ballerina. Your papa had returned to see his own mother and came to spend Christmas with us. You followed him everywhere. We went to visit her several times. She had a dog. The garden was a mess.'

She puts the photograph back down on the table and starts looking through the other papers that are in front of her. The conversation's over. It's no wonder I can't remember things if she doesn't talk to me. I pick the photo up and take it upstairs to my own room. I count to thirty by the time I turn the handle to my door. Sitting in the corner of my sofa closest to the radiator I switch on the reading lamp. I want to remember this picture. I want to smell it and see it and feel it and I'm dizzy with the effort. I need to know who took the photograph, and what was in the present sitting in front of me.

Closing my eyes I can vaguely see a small girl in a stiff orange dress, twirling around with her arms above her head. I can smell stew and beer and the fire in the grate. There's music playing, it's not Christmas music, or maybe it is. My mum is laughing and happy I can't see who else is there. There's a knock at the front door and I run to open it. A strange man is standing there. He's tall and different to the usual people who come to our house. He's white. My mum's behind me and I feel the stillness that's come into the hallway with her. I don't know what she says but she isn't happy anymore. Then the man's picking me up and carrying me into the kitchen and he's loud and doesn't fit into the room properly.

Opening my eyes, I look out into the bare garden. There's a robin on the tree at the back. I take out the bleach and begin to wash the kitchen cupboard fronts. The photograph is waiting for me on the coffee table.

All my presents are wrapped, the tree is downstairs waiting, the food is packed into our fridges. Kutes is out and my mum's busy with her memories. In two weeks and four days we'll be in Nigeria to bury my dad.

I pick up the photo that is still waiting. It's clearer now. There was an uncle in the kitchen with us. I don't know which uncle. Everyone who came was greeted as uncle or aunty by me. In turn their children called my mum aunty. It's what we did. It was this uncle who took the picture. Dad's big voice insisting, Mum saying she was too busy. I wanted to open the present he had brought with him. Mum wouldn't let me. She gave me a slap round the back of my head. It didn't hurt because my hair was in big bunches with orange ribbons to match my dress.

Uncle took my hand and said we were going for a walk but I didn't want to. There were raised voices and I hid between the corner and the sideboard. My dad's voice was big and my mum was just as loud. All I could see were shadows dancing around the room. My mum's with her hands conducting and my dad's slumped and shuffling around. I saw uncle pass by as he went to the kitchen door and I heard it close softly behind him. The argument carried on for a long time and some of it was about me. My dad wanted to take me back to Nigeria with him but my mum refused. I can't remember anything else, but dad didn't stay for Christmas dinner and I didn't get my present. Maybe that's what happened.

Kutes is in the hallway. She's laughing at something. I haven't heard her laugh for a while.

'Hi Kutes, are you all right?'

'Err, I'm on the phone. What are you doing under the table?'

'Cleaning.'

Kutes flounces off and stomps upstairs.

I go and sit on the sofa with a throw wrapped round me. I had a lot of uncles when I was little. What is it about parents when they insist that every man they see is your uncle? Maybe I'm being unfair. I'm sure there weren't that many. It's not like there's anything worth remembering from my childhood. Except playing out. The best times were hanging out at Alex Park. Near the lake there was a rockery. It was like a secret world. There'd be people all around, feeding the ducks and sitting on benches with babies in prams. I'd have to wait for the exact right moment, when the parky had passed with his dog. And then sneak into the bushes. It wasn't even a rockery, that's just what we called it.

The trees and bushes were so thick nobody would know you were there. You could spy on people, but we only did that if there was someone having an argument or kissing. Most times we went on adventures.

Once I ran away from home straight to the rockery. I had a blanket and some limeade. I don't remember why I ran away. I must have been about eleven I suppose. The earth and pond smells were comforting. It was always damp and dank in there, the shrubbery never disturbed except by the occasional duck looking for a nesting space. I collected the soft feathers that were stuck on the leaves. It was Dia that found me. She stayed with me for another hour until it was dark. We told stories and threw pebbles at ducks in the water. She didn't even ask me what was wrong. I'd forgotten about that.

Kutes

You nearly ready carls
Yeah yeah just gotta straighten me hair
Xmas eve yeah and shes tryin to get me to stay in an decorate the fuckin xmas tree
Hahahahahahahahahaha
Like thats gonna happen I aint 6 next shell be telling me about father xmas
Nah its nice to do that stuff tho innit just not when uve got a party to go to haha
Its nice if yer mum aint a fuckin nutta an yer nan aint losin her marbles
Hey its xmas give em a break lol
Woteva you heard her when I was walkin past her room dint ya
Yeah she sounded alrite from what I could tell she only asked yer how ya was an you like only stopped chattin to me for a sec an I cud just imagine the look on yer face hahahahahaha
Yeah but its like obvious im on the phone innit then this smell of bleach hits me an me eyes start waterin an the lot an shes under the table scrubbin
Hahahahahahahahahahahahaha nah kutes dont be so harsh its xmas innit
Yeah I suppose but then I goes down to say hiya to me nan and shes like showin me old fashioned pictures an shit an I aint fuckin interested when ive got to get ready tho she had a proper cool hat on in one of em
Hahahahahahahahahaha your bad ya know
Anyways is wahida comin out she was proper down yesterday
Yeah yeah spoke to her before so hurry up
Inabit

Ade

I do not know if I made the correct decision at the time, but it has turned out well. My family are under this roof once more. It was difficult at the time, sha! I did not really know what I had decided to do but I had felt it was the correct decision.

At first when Mrs Kingsley left I did not move my belongings downstairs. Somehow it would have been wrong. Each morning I would rise before 5.30 a.m. and take my bath and then go downstairs quickly. I wanted everything to be as it was before. So I would have the kitchen door slightly ajar and listen out for the students coming downstairs. Eh-heh! What a silly child I was, thinking that those boys would treat me as they had Mrs Kingsley.

On the first morning they had appeared for their breakfast oats and although I had watched many times how to cook it I had never before done it alone. What I placed in the bowls in front of them was terrible. A grey lump that looked more like eba than porridge oats. These boys did not even pretend to try and eat it and one of them stood his spoon in the middle and it stayed upright. I was beside myself and did not know what to do. They teased me terribly and I did not think that was respectful as I was their landlady now. For a long time, when each student arrived to my house they would be warned of my morning oats, although by then I had learnt to cook them well. In fact, I had spent one whole day cooking pan after pan of oats, each time throwing away a disaster and scrubbing the pan out with wire wool. I was in tears by the end of that day but I learned.

I was very concerned that I did everything correctly so for some weeks I did not have time to think about what my future would be. One morning when James came to visit I was feeling sickly. He made the porridge while I sat and sipped water. He convinced me that I should move into the downstairs rooms, pointing at the slight roundness that was beginning to show behind my apron. That same day I lost our second baby. I was only six weeks gone so this was not as traumatic as the first time.

James began to treat my house as though it was his own, inviting people to have meetings in my kitchen. It was only by watching and listening carefully that I discovered what he was doing. Oh, it was nothing very exciting. Back home I had believed he was important-o. Once I was here, I could see how my own people were studying so hard to be lawyers or doctors and yet James was still running around the streets thinking he was a big man.

Am I being cruel? I do not think so. Olu told me that James was typical working class. That's what he said exactly. Typical working class. I did not know what that meant at the time, and now I do not think that I agree. James made money. He talked and he met and he agitated in the right places at the right time for him to get something out of it. I am sure now he would be called an entrepreneur. He would be thinking up ideas and going on to the television to sell them to the world. It took me a while to understand that the times he spent in my room were the times when things had not gone as he planned.

I had thought that after the conference everything would stop, as is the way with men and their ideas, but it appeared to me that this had been a serious gathering. At the beginning I refused to take the notes for James's meetings because I was angry that he felt he could use my home in this way. But as the meetings progressed and I heard what was being said I became more interested. Change was happening. In Africa and in all the countries who had raised a flag at our conference. My students were becoming involved. I had one student from the Gold Coast, one from South Africa and I think maybe one or two from Kenya, I am not too sure now. Of course, all of the students who stayed in my house were some years older than me. And I was their landlady. Many times I had to pinch myself to believe that it was true. I would write letters to Funmi telling her of the things I was doing. She would write me back of how I was now a big woman.

I was worried about my family back home. Funmi advised me of the situation in our village. Papa had not returned home after I left and other men had disappeared including Uncle Tunde. Other fathers had also disappeared. Many of the women were having a hard time feeding their children. Mama had begun to walk to the big tree outside the village more often than before. Funmi had witnessed a meeting of the village women on more than one occasion, although she could not report to me about what they were speaking. I had to urge her in one of my letters to move close enough so that she could tell me what was being said.

Finally, I received a letter from her that made my heart rise. Mama was organising the women to fend for themselves, keep their houses in order and to share what little resources they could find amongst each other. In our own compound Mama had a store of food that she was sharing with some of the poorer women who had many children, but aunty had been making trouble and saying that it should be kept for our compound only.

I did not understand how affairs had become so bad in our village but I understood that the situation was being repeated throughout our country. This is what I had learned from the meetings I attended right here in Manchester. Things I would not have known had I still been in my compound. Imagine. I travel to the other side of the world and learn more about my own country than I could have known before.

When I tell James what is happening in my village he becomes quite agitated and asks many questions about the men that I do not have the answers for.

'So what of your Papa, Ade? Is he well?'

'Papa has not returned since before we left, James, we do not know where he is.'

'Oh, I'm sure he's fine, probably got another family somewhere.'

'How can you say that about my papa? He would not do that to my mama. Did you see him being polygamous when you drove him around? No I did not think so.'

He leaves the room in a hurry.

I was a landlady but I knew that I had to earn more than what the tenants were paying to me. I learned to sew. Sheila spent one afternoon with me on Mrs. Kingsley's old Singer that she had left behind and I became an expert on the sewing machine sha! I started with tablecloths and towels. Soon I was able to do linings in coats.

The conference had told a lot of our young men that they had to learn much before they returned home. If our countries were going to become independent they would need to replace the white man in his job. I did not understand how law or business or anything that involved writing and talking all day would help to produce food for people. But of course there were engineers and other such people who would return to manage and run the machines that would be left behind when the white man left our countries. What a thing we imagined at that time, sha!

I was still working at Mr Konnen's restaurant, but I was also looking for other work. Olu came to eat one Saturday evening and we walked home together afterwards. He was full of ideas, as excited about the conference as though it was happening right then. Big ideas. Too many for one man. All he wanted to do was talk-talk. I listened to him as much as I could. He did not require answers, just ears. Stopping underneath one lamp, he turned to me. He was so tall-o I had to tilt up my head to look at his face. And I thought he was going to kiss me. But he simply smiled at me with such a look on his face I did not know what to do.

'How-now, Ade?' he said to me and my legs turned to river water and my skin prickled like it had too much sun. And all he had said to me was 'how-now, Ade'. When we are young we are very foolish. To find love under a lamp-post in a darkened Manchester park does not happen. But at that time I believed I had found it and my mouth refused to work to give him any answer. He did not seem to notice how I was feeling, he just took my arm and tucked it under his and continued walking and talking. I was in a state of confusion and had not even told him any of my plans. But right at that moment I believed that I had travelled all the way to Manchester to meet this man.

I waited for him to give me one piece of hope that he had felt something under that lamp-post. He found time to ask me about my college studies, but did not really give me time to answer before he started telling me of his plans once he reached the Bar. I did not know which bar he was talking of and asked him. He laughed at me. My river legs became firm again. How was I supposed to know about something I had never heard of. I took my arm from his and walked ahead to my house. I did not invite him in.

Hei, do I have time to make this reminiscent trip when I have food to prepare? Why would I remember this Olu? I married James. Oh, it was not easy to be with him, coming and going. And we lost so many babies I did not expect to bring one child into this world. And look now I have my daughter and my granddaughter.

Elizabeth

When I was little this house scared me. It was all creaks and grumbles and feet walking around upstairs. I slept in the front room downstairs, where my mum still sleeps. There was just the one big bed, metal frame and a sagging mattress and I would sleep right in the centre of it until my mum came to bed and moved me to one side. I didn't know that my friends didn't sleep in their parents' room, I thought it was normal. The door to the bedroom leads straight off from the kitchen, next to the big dresser and the same curtain's still hanging over it. Sometimes I had to sleep on a mattress on the floor.

Dia is asleep next to me in my bed on the first floor and it couldn't be more different if it tried. I need Nigeria to be over. I hate the way I'm thinking and remembering.

Kutes

hey kutes hows it goin
      I swear I've still got a hangover from xmas
      Lols me too xmas eve was the best
      And xmas night
      And boxing night hahaha anyways wots up
      i seriously cant stand it carls i swear I cant
      tell yer aunty carly all about it
      its nearly the fuckin 10th innit 1 fuckin day to go
      come on kutes it aint that bad at least itll be ova an done wiv
      it aint bad for you but it aint you thats goin
      kk lets think bout some positives yeah
      hmmmmmm nope cant think of any
      jeez yr not much fun are ya
      ive not even packed yet
      ill come round 18a if u want an help ya gotta do all yer sexy outfits innit
      yer rite cos they do sexy in a fuckin village
      youll show em how hahahahahahahahaha
      come round im depressed
      giv us an hour yeah

Ade

When I arrived I had one small brown box. In it were two English blouses and skirts. The rest of the room was taken with my wrappers. Funmi had hidden something in there for me but I cannot remember what it was. Oh, yes. Money. She had hidden money because she knew I would need it.

On my final evening before I left home to be with James, I walked through each room and touched everything. It did not help me to return. In the living area the furniture, which had been so fine, was fading with a fine layer of red dust covering the cabinets and the small ornaments that my mama loved so. Funmi and I fetched a damp rag and began to wipe everything down so that it shone as it should. We tidied the cushions on the sofas and beat the rugs outside. Funmi swept the floors and we were pleased with our work. Mama did not even notice. I thought that she was not so impressed with our work. Funmi and I had talked long into the night about my return and I had not even left. We planned out the changes we would make when I was earning so much money. But I did not return as planned and Funmi married and had her daughter and I married and had my daughter and life did not turn out as we planned at all.

There is something happening in this house that I do not like. I am sure that my daughter is inviting it with her ways. I do not have time for such things. What is a mother to do, sha? Did I ask for this child? How so am I supposed to arrange her if she will not be arranged? See how my mind is wandering now. How many babies did I lose before Elizabeth came along? It was five or six, I forget now. Even after we married the babies could not stay. This is why I did not return home. How would I have told my own mama that I could not even keep hold of the thing that made me leave? But Elizabeth came. She stayed inside me.

Hah! Never mind all of that now. Today I shall walk through this house as I have not done for many years.

'Mum, what are you doing?'

'I am taking one walk around my house, daughter, will you not accompany me?'

'You can't do the stairs, mum, what do you want to walk around for?'

'Did I ask you to question me so? It is still my house and I shall walk around it as I please.'

'Hang on I'll get Kutes.'

'Nan, you alright? Why're ya sitting on the stairs?'

'I am fine thank you very much. I am simply resting. I will take a walk around.'

'Mum we've got to get ready, we haven't got time for this right now.'

'Is it so, Elizabeth? Did I ask for your assistance?'

Aiy aiy aiy! What a distance those stairs are now. I am sure they have lengthened over the years. Perhaps this house is stretching as I am shrinking.

'Do you know that when I arrived there was carpet all the way through, from the bottom of those stairs until the bottom of the ones at the other end of this corridor. Aha! This room here, this one. This is where that cheeky young man stayed. My first student. Now what was his name-o?'

'Nan, I've not finished packing yet I need to go upstairs.'

'Samuel. Yes, it was Samuel. What a fine young man he was. Studying every day coming home for some dinner and then off again in the evenings to work down the mines. We had mines you know, right here in Manchester. This boy Samuel, he worked very hard. Do you know at first when he arrived he would sneak his books into his room? He did not think that I would go and sweep when he was out and see what he was reading. The books he had piled up in this corner here all about trade union and communism. So I invited him to one meeting we were holding downstairs and he did not know what type of meeting it was. Hei! The look on his face when he realised that he was with his comrades.'

'So you were really a commie, nan? A real one?'

'What is this commie? We were fighting for our freedom. Does that make us have one label? I do not think so.'

Elizabeth

'Come on Mum, I'll help you downstairs. You shouldn't have done this. Not before we travel. What's the matter with you? We'll be coming back, you know we will.'

It's not as though she's never been around the house before, I'm sure she was up and down those stairs when the builders were in. Dia will be here soon and I wanted to have a chilled afternoon with her and I know Kutes will be going to see Carly, so it's my time.

'Yes I know your room was in the attic, Mum, you've told us so many times. I'm not being impatient it's just that you know we're travelling tomorrow. You could have come up any time. Yes, I know it was 1945 when you came, Mum. And it was Dad who brought you.'

Kutes

I am gonna fuckin scream in a minit wot are they doin its not fair why should I have to put up with this shit I swear I aint goin nowhere with them two but if I dont go summatll happen to em both an then Ill feel guilty for the rest of me life it aint fuckin fair why cant I just have a normal life like carls whyve I got a mental mum

Ade

'Ah, so many of my boys passed through these rooms and all of them had such respect. This house was where they all wanted to be. They would travel home and the next lot of students would arrive on my doorstep with a note from the previous ones. I had quite a waiting list at one time. There were not so many accommodating landladies back then. In fact, I am sure that at one time there were uprisings in the streets about the houses that took in African students. Yes, we had many meetings about that-o. This is a very nice bathroom. Perhaps I should bring myself up here occasionally to enjoy such luxury.'

'I offered to do your bathroom up Mum, you know I did.'

'The first time I walked along this corridor I was frightened. I did not think that the house would stand for long and it became so dark the further I travelled. What a silly young girl I was. Look now, it is light and the corner is not so far away.'

'Yer not goin' into my room, Nan.'

'Is it so? You are forbidding me to enter a room in my own home?'

'She didn't mean that, Mum, she just means that the stairs might be too much for you.'

'Hmph! We shall see about these stairs. They did not have carpet when I arrived. Just to the bottom stair it went and then finished. Now it is the opposite way around. Modernisation I suppose it must be. And this banister has become loose. Do you know this is one of the first things I had put into the house when I bought it? I did not want any other person to suffer walking up here with nothing to hold on to as I did when I arrived. I felt sure I would fall to my death. You child, need to have your cough attended to, you do not want to be sick when we travel. Let me just sit a while here.'

'We really have to go now Mum, Dia'll be here in a minute and I've got to finish off downstairs.'

'It is very warm in here now. And that window has changed. When it was mine it could open all the way out and I could lean over and see almost to the park. How do you move around in here with all of this furniture and what's all this on the floor? Did I not teach you to keep your belongings in one place? Look at all the cupboards and wardrobes you have and still you find place on the floor for books and clothes.'

'Woteva, I'm sure I just heard the door.'

'So many changes. Is this still my house? I will rest a while.'

Elizabeth

'Mum, you're not listening. I've got stuff to do. Why would you want to be sitting up here? This room is disgusting. It needs cleaning or it'll stink the whole house out before we get back.'

I have no idea why I'm saying this stuff to her. I'm never going to be able to get her downstairs on my own. She's gone into that other world. I'm sure she's got dementia coming on. Oh, shit, I can't stand it. What the hell am I going to do with her in Nigeria?

'Aunty Dia's downstairs can we get out of me room now, please?'

I should have had a skylight put in at this corner. You can't leave doors open like this, they need to hold their stories and ghosts inside and now they're all out.

'Hey babes, come here, what's up?'

'I need to clean before we leave.'

'It's so clean my nostrils are burning.'

'I have to do a bit more. It's going to be empty for a week and I don't want germs to start growing.'

'Ya know what, Beth, I think you're bonkers and when you come back we need to get this sorted out.'

And this time she's not joking, I can see it in her eyes.

'You need to get a grip. It's not healthy for you or anyone else around you. I'm trying really hard just now because I know you're stressed, but honestly, I've about had enough. I'll go and make a brew, then I'll sort your mum out.'

There's no point saying anything to her. My chest hurts.

When I was eleven there was a woman living in here. She was a bit strange and always smelled of damp earth. She didn't have a name and she scared me, but I couldn't stay away from her. It was as though she called me and I had to come. There was lino down in the rooms back then, with just a thin rug in the middle. She'd be sitting down, in the centre of the mat and she'd make me sit opposite her. I don't remember her coming to our house and I don't remember her leaving. My mum can't remember her at all. But she was here. She had deep brown eyes that at times would seem to be the only features in her face, and she was old, incredibly old. Her skin was stretched and dry and her fingers that were long and bony were covered in red dust. She wore the same wrapper every time I saw her. I don't know how many times I saw her because I didn't count back then. Her hair was so closely cropped that I could see her scalp and when I was standing up I saw bald patches at the back of her head.

I should have been frightened but I wasn't. She didn't want to hurt me, she wanted to tell me things. Her voice was like a million trees blowing in an autumn wind. It rustled through her chest and came out like a whispered howl, 'Adeola, what is this that you are doing?' And I wanted to protest, to tell her that my name wasn't Adeola, but I didn't want her to stop talking to me. And besides I wasn't doing anything, I was just sitting. I haven't thought about her for years. In fact, I forgot all about her. Maybe this is a sign. Maybe she's telling me not to go.

'Mum what ya doin?'

'What? I'm not doing anything, I'm cleaning.'

'No, yer sittin cross legged in the middle of yer room like a friggin buddah.'

She's right.

'You have to lock your door. And make sure the window's closed, ok?'

'Jeez, we're only goin for a week innit, an whose gonna be comin through my window its on the friggin roof.'

'Right, your mum's downstairs, I've made her a cup of tea and her cases are by the door ready. What are you doing?'

'Exactly, that's what I said, she's off her head.'

'Oi, young lady, don't talk about your mum like that, go and sit with your nan and make sure she doesn't start doing anything else.'

'And Kutes?'

'Yes?'

'Don't flounce, love.'

So simple, their relationship. If that was me saying it we'd have a stand up argument and she's be slamming doors and ignoring everything I said. Maybe I'm not really her mum, maybe Dia is and we forgot.

'Right, we need to sort out some food. Are you all right? Do I need to get you anything?'

'There was an old woman who lived here. I used to sit with her like this and she'd tell me things.'

'What things Beth? When did she live here? Was she one of your mum's tenants?'

'I can't remember. She was very old.'

'We can ask your mum about her, can't we?'

'But it might be a sign. That we shouldn't be going. I haven't thought about her since I was a child and now I'm thinking about her and maybe it's a sign.'

But I know Dia isn't understanding anything I'm saying and I don't really believe it's a sign, if it was it would be like in a film and I'd get a flashback and everything would be really clear and I'd have the answer to what I needed and everything would turn out all right. I really do need to get a grip.

Kutes

Im gunna go mad wid thm
    innit ther nutttas
    txt bk
    jeez kutes its 5 in the am
    wer u at
    airport innit bin ere 4 an hour in a bit ill text yer before we bord
    kk

'Mum I'm gonna have a look around.'
    'Ok, but don't go far, I'm sure we'll be going to the gate soon.'
    'Ah granddaughter, I will come with you. I have one small gift to buy.'
    'Nah, changed me mind, I'm gonna wait here.'

no fukin chnce wid dese 2 its not fair
    haha wot hppned
    me fukin nan wanted to cum wid innit

hahaha dont be tite mite of worked innit like u woz takin old ladies out
for a trip all kind an carin an shit

yh rite u cum an try it shes dressed in all big prints an headraps an shit its
enuff that ive gotta sit near em
    hahahaha u giv me joke txt me b4 yer plane leaves

149

Ade

What a journey, hei! So many people are travelling home. And would you believe I met Mrs Akeji's daughter. What a fine woman she has become. It was so long ago she would sit beside the fire in my kitchen, reading her books, while we, the adults, debated and argued. Ten years since her mother passed, still a young woman. But what a joy to see her daughter travelling home with her own children.

Was that food they served to us on our journey? I do not think so. Small foil containers with dried to the edges potatoes, which I am sure were made from powder.And now we have arrived and they want this old lady to walk down a metal stairway that is swinging this way and that just like when I boarded the ship so long ago, but then I was young. How so? Where is the bridge that we walked down to come into the aeroplane? Ah, but this heat. It is wrapping me like one of the tartan blankets my daughter insists that I need. Yes, we are home. Now my aching body can be as it should.

So busy. All the time moving, moving. It was not like this when Elizabeth was ten and we travelled here. What a good girl she was, colouring her books and not one complaint. Unlike those children of Mrs Akeji. Up and down. Questions, questions. Did she not teach them right?

'Mum are you ok?'

'I am fine daughter. Are you well?'

'Yes, we're just waiting for the bags. We're over there, ok?'

Hei, that daughter of mine with her worries and concerns. Such a strange child she has always been. It is good to see my brothers and sisters around me. And soon I shall be with Funmi, dear, dear Funmi.

'Nan, are yer with us? We're goin now.'

'Mum, this man's going to take us through. Can you walk?'

'Did I not walk before? What man is this?'

'Aunty Funmi's daughter sent him, just give him the passports, please.'

So this is how it has become. It takes a man to bring me into my own country. Perhaps we did not fight hard enough all those years ago. Or perhaps I am too English now and have forgotten how it is. But wait, is that not Funmi waiting for us? It is not possible, she could not have remained the same.

'Ma, you are welcome. Did you journey well?'

'Funmi?'

'No, Mum, it's Aunty Funmi's granddaughter.'

'Hei, look at you. Yes we are well. How now, daughter?'

'Ma we have a car waiting for you, will I help?'

'Ah, what a good girl you are, just like my sister, Funmi.'

Imagine a car waiting. And it is a nice car. But it is so dark out here. And look at the airport, so big and majestic with its lights.

'What time is it daughter?'

'It is past seven, Ma. We shall soon be home. Mama has prepared food for you.'

'Elizabeth, did you collect all of our luggages?'

'Yes, Mum.'

I have so many gifts for my sister Funmi. It is good to be home. Perhaps I will take a bath and sleep before anything else. Is this stupid driver trying to kill us all? How can he know which way to go, it is so dark? Hei, and these roads.

'Will you tell the driver to be more careful?'

'Sorry Ma, but we are arriving now.'

'So you can see in the dark now, is it?'

Ah-ha. I see the lights, but wait. This is a high wall. And a man to open the gates.

'You are welcome, Ma, may I help you?'

'Heh, I do not think I have one solid bone left to walk with.'

'Mama is waiting for you inside.'

'This house is big. And you have one generator?'

'Come on, Mum, I haven't got any repellent on. Kutes take her handbag.'

'I can carry my own bag. Have you ever seen a house such as this one. And a generator. Imagine.'

'Ade, is it you?

'Eh-eh! Funmi is it you? Did you grow so old and fat?'

'What a thing to say-o. Can you not see me well? And you, you have grown old and skinny.'

Ah, it is good to be home. So long since I have seen my dear sister.

'Ade, what you dey do? Is it time to cry?'

'Who said I was crying? Am I not just tired from the journey-o?'

But she smells of our past. Her shoulder is as comforting as it always was. Her arms tell me everything will be well. This is too much for an old lady to bear. Why did I not return home before? Was it through shame?

Now I must not think in this way. I did not leave my mama with no one to care for her. Funmi was there.

'Mum, what's wrong? Please don't do this. You should be happy to be here.'

'Go and put your bag in your room, child. Your mama, she is fine.'

Funmi is still looking after me. I have missed this so much yet I was not aware of it until right now. She is my own true sister.

'I am all right. It is so much to be here with you again after all this time.'

'Hush now, Ade, we will be well. Come, eat.'

'Eh-heh! Is this Gbagba? I have not made this dish since I left-o. You could always make this better than me. The cray fish does not taste this fine when it has travelled all the way to England. And I am sure we do not have the correct melon. But pepper we can always get. Pepper does not alter its taste when it journeys.'

The food is good, although we should not be eating so late, I am sure. My gari has never come out as well as Funmi's, even though Mama taught us both well.

'Ade, you are falling asleep in your stew. Come, we have prepared your bed.'

'You are still looking after me, sister. What of Elizabeth and Kutes?'

'They have gone to sleep already, Ade. Come now.'

In the lamplight she looks like my Funmi from before. She takes my arm as though I am an old lady and she is my daughter. My body is too tired.

'A-hah! NEPA! Still this is happening, here in big Lagos?'

'Even up to Abujah, Ade. Imagine, we can supply electricity for so many countries, but here we have to go without. What a thing-o.'

'But the generator will work?'

'Not until we have been in our beds for a few hours. We do not want to attract armed robbers who think that we have more than them. My son-in-law is a very smart man.'

'Ma, I have a torch, please come with me. I have drawn water for your bath.'

'Such good girls you have Funmi. Goodnight, my dear.'

Elizabeth

Oh, god, the journey was a nightmare. Kutes sulked all the way and Mum was sniffing at people, pulling her face and sucking her teeth.

At the airport, she looked so old and frail. Sweat was pouring down her face. Then she's acting like there's nothing wrong. I don't know if I can look after her and Kutes and bury my dad. It's too much to deal with. But Aunty Funmi will look after Mum. I don't need to worry about it. So why am I still thinking? We're in Funmi's house. We're safe.

Ten. Ten. Ten. I don't want to open my eyes. It's too hot and I dread to think about the creatures that are crawling around the walls. I'm sticky. Everything is sticky. I think I may be sick. Perhaps I was bitten last night.

'Sistah, are you awake yet?'

If I keep my eyes closed she'll go away. Funmi's daughter, my second cousin. Stood right next to me. I can smell her.

'Oh, hi, Yetunde, what time is it?'

'It is past eight, I thought perhaps you would like to shower in my own bathroom.'

'A shower would be lovely, I'm sticky. It's really hot. Do you know where Kutes is?'

'She has gone out with my daughter to the shops.'

Kutes up and out of the house at eight in the morning, that's unheard of. The floor. It's lino. And it's old. And I just can't.

'Okay, I'll get up now, which one's your bathroom?'

'Straight across. I have left a towel and some soap for you. My husband brought it from London, I am sure you will like it.'

My towel is on the top of my clothes in the suitcase. I'm glad I put it in a plastic bag, I can still smell the Lenor. The blue one. And there's no dust. The bathroom is pale pink. With blue mats and shower curtain.

It isn't en suite, although they could easily knock through. Bleach. There's bleach under the sink. There's Vim too. Haha! Vim. Wait until I tell Dia. Vim and Ajax have disappeared at home.

Now I can shower.

'Sistah, are you fine? Is everything fine?'

'Yeah, won't be long.'

These stairs are marble. Maybe I could wear sandals while I'm here, but no, I don't think so.

'Morning, Mum, morning, Aunt Funmi.'

'Ah, Elizabeth, did you sleep well?'

'Yes, thanks, Mum, did you? You were still chatting when Kutes and I went up last night.'

'We shall eat eggs for breakfast, with English toast, or so the girl tells me, hah!'

'Hear this Funmi-o, talking like a bush girl. So you don't know toast, hei?'

'Mum that's not nice.'

I swear she's getting senile. Anything can come out of her mouth at any time. It's not good.

'Are you not too warm dressed with so many clothes, daughter?'

'No I'm fine, the air-conditioning works well. My pants are almost like cheese cloth and my top's cotton.'

'Did I not say so, Funmi? This one of mine has funny ways, sha!'

'And she's sat at the table next to you, Mum, so perhaps you'd like to not talk about her like that.'

'Eh-heh! What is this, now?'

'It's nothing aunty, I just brought my own fork, I prefer to use my own stuff.'

'Ade, I think you have done right to bring your children home. Maybe you waited too long.'

The eggs are nice.

'Did Kutes eat before she went out? Has she gone far?'

I hope she dressed properly, none of that skimpy stuff. I should have checked her suitcase. She might attract too much attention. What if something happens to her?

'Do you think we would not take care of our own daughter? She is well. Ade, we must have a serious talk when we arrive home.'

'What do you mean arrive home? Are you coming back to Manchester with us?'

'What a question. When we go home to Sapele.'

Kutes

No way carls, u wont believe it its like fuckin amazing here in Naija. My cousin brought me to an internet caff an I cant get on messenger so that's why I'm mailin yer – u betta get this and reply cos I no what you're like with mails.

Rite, we got off the plane and it's a great big bloody airport with shops and everything and this guy comes and gets our passports and I thought like shit is he nickin em or wot and anyways he just walks us through customs like we was royalty or summat.

It's so friggin hot even at nite and its pitch black and we were in this beat up old car that was sent for us but before we got in it yeah there's like loads of sweaty guys pushing in to get our bags and shit like on a movie or summat, and me mum's like getting all tight and panicking and she's got them owl eyes she does and me nan's like stood with this daft smile on her face like she's seen jesus or summat and the guy that met us rushes up and talks to these sweatys dead ruff an they like do one quick.

So anyways we're in Lagos now which used to be the capital but now it isn't which is weird cos I didn't know you could move a capital city and me nan always said Lagos was the capital but obvs she was wrong!!! It aint much to look at really but it's dead busy – we walked from the house where we're staying and the side roads are like weird more like dirt tracks only red lol! And then ya just like go round a corner an you're in a main street that's like got too many people and cars and bus things like vans really and people are hanging out of em and did I tell ya its only like seven thirty in the morning yeah and I'm up an out hahahahaha!

Anyways the house we're staying in is wicked it's got a wall round it an gates with a doorman an everything or is that a gateman dunno – its probably a bit posh but not to us cos it just looks like dusty and things thrown into it – its nice still

And get this yeah I'm wearing like an African top thing cos I put me cutoffs on with that white vest top that we got from top shop yeah and me belly ring was showing and looking buff but me nan's sister, I think it is anyways, so that makes her me great aunty or summat, she like starts laughing at me when I went downstairs and she was looking at me belly ring and she liked it yeah it's the silver one with the red stone an the dangly diamond bits and she starts telling me some story about when she woz young yeah and rituals and shit but I couldn't be arsed listening so like Funke that's the one who's here with me yeah she like sees me face and goes and gets this top and its dead cool I mite bring yer one back so we can start a new fashion its like cut dead simple like a vest yeah but its got this cross over flap thing at the front so it covers me up but if I turn round quick the flap opens and ya get a flash of me belly ring we woz proper laughing bout it when we come out cos if I hadn't put it on Funmi would've kept me there forever lol.

I think me times nearly up now but I'll send you another mail later I think we're going to the countryside anyways so I hope there's some internet there better bloody had be and I think I'm gonna get me hair done like Funke's when we go to a market its dead cool really tiny plaits and she says it only takes a couple of hours. Can't wait bet the markets are buzzing.

Do ya want me to bring ya sumthin native back I'll see wot I can find anyways mite get ya a voodoo doll hahahahahahahahah

K

Ps don't laugh at the way I'm writing, Funke was going on about the fact that we don't learn anything in school cos I can't talk and write proper so I had to show her lols. Don't worry I'll be back to normal by the time I get back. Laters

Ade

It is so good to be here. This heat is already easing the pain in my hip. After lunch we shall travel to Benin to pay our respects. I do not know how that stupid wife will react, but this is how it will be.

I am happy that Funmi has returned to Sapele. Benin is no place to live for a woman of her age. Hei, what am I saying? Are we not almost age mates? I will like to walk by the river again. It will be good to show the children how far we have all travelled.

'Funmi, my sister, did I not write you of Elizabeth's strange ways?'

'Not to worry, Ade, we shall cure her while she is with us.'

'What is there to cure? It is the way she is. Perhaps I did not do my job so well. Always there were meetings to hold. A house to run. Perhaps I should not have left her to grow up alone. James told me I should come home.'

'Pah! What did James know about where you should be? If it had not been for James you would have become a great lawyer, so we shall not talk about what James told you, sha!'

'Ah, Funmi, our dreams. Did I waste them? I tried so hard to go to school, but it was too difficult for women. And for coloureds. Can you imagine, that is what I was called. Coloured. I did not know until I was told, I believed I was Ade.'

'They have very strange ways in London. Coloured! But you did well Ade, I have seen the photographs of your great house. And I have met some of your tenants over the years who have given me stories of you. Especially that Olu.'

'Olu? My Olu? Hei, what am I saying? Is he here? I have not spoken to him for ten years or more.'

'He is in Warri, with one fine house. And his wife passed, you know. I did not like her very much with her English ways.'

'She passed? Ah, poor Olu, although I am sure more were ready to take her place.'

'Oh, no, Ade, he is waiting for you!'

The last time I saw Olu, he looked fine and handsome. He had retired from his law business in London and had travelled to visit his friends in Manchester. When I opened the door and saw him standing in my porch, I thought my heart would stop. He looked so good. When his wife stepped up beside him and put her arm through his I felt him move away from me inside, although he still smiled he tipped his head so that the hat he was wearing hid his eyes. It was a difficult meeting and his wife did not allow any conversation unless she directed the topic. Yes, we are retiring back home. Yes, we have built a beautiful house in Warri, just off Sapele Road. Yes, our children are very well. We have three you know, and seven grandchildren, yes, they will be coming to visit. Hah! Olu looked up then and we shared a moment because we knew that there were eight grandchildren. She did not need to know this.

Olu did not want to leave and he held my hand for a long time. His wife was not pleased. And now she has gone. So I have come to bury one husband and I shall perhaps see the one who should have been mine.

'Have you gone to the river, Ade? Our driver has arrived-o! We are going home.'

'Eh-heh! Did I sleep? Are my children here?'

'Mum we're here. I've taken the bags to the car. Are you ok?'

'Where is Kutes? Did she return? Ah, there you are daughter. We shall go to visit your grandfather.'

'Yeah, Nan, whatever. Not really up for visiting deads. I hope there's air conditioning in the car. I like it in Lagos, do I have to come?'

'Now we are going home.'

'Whatever.'

The car is not as I expected it to be. It is large and I am not sure I will be able to step up to it. What is that child saying? Toyota? What is Toyota? Ah it is the type of car. Of course I have seen it being advertised. The driver is on the wrong side. It does not smell of Nigeria inside. Although I can only put my head in.

'Am I to step up into this? Do you think my knees are young?'

'Wait, Ade, the children will bring my plastic step.'

'Ah, so I am not the only one who has a problem-o.'

Hei! I feel like the queen sat up here. I am tired. This city is different. I do not understand why those children are dressed in knicker and look so dirty, there across the road. Do their mother's not hold shame? They are living in Lagos! It is like a slum here. Like South Africa. Like shanty town.

'What is this area called, Funmi? I do not care for it.'

'Ade, perhaps you should rest your mouth for a while.'

She is right. What is happening to me? I do not complain and moan like a grumpy old woman. Why are they taking so long to load our luggages? These people-o. They must discuss everything without doing any action and still they will have a problem fixing things.

'Elizabeth will you arrange the boxes before we are meeting nightfall?'

'It's being done Mum, it's fine. There's a lot of luggage.'

'You see, Funmi? What this England does to our children.'

'Ade close your eyes and close your mouth. I do not remember you to be so miserable.'

'Pah!'

Finally, we are moving. This place is so higgledy-piggledy. How do people know where they live? I do not wonder they removed the capital to Abuja. Look at these children running in between cars selling their goods. I wonder how many will return home with their few kobo tonight. It is better for me to close my eyes.

I will meet with Olu. Perhaps. Maybe he has travelled. Maybe his children and grandchildren are with him. I am sure he must have a woman. Ten years. Would I have contacted him if I had known? But he did not contact me. I remember the first time I set eyes on him. I had not been in Manchester for more than three hours. He looked so handsome framed in the door with the sun pouring in behind him. He looked just like the pictures of angels with haloes. Or did he? Was it not raining when I arrived? Was it not night time? My feet were wet and my coat stank.

He was so cheeky to me that I thought I hated him. James hated him. If I had not married James, I am sure it would have been Olu. Sha! What am I thinking? His eyes smiled all the time, even when he was angry about his politics. When we walked through Alexandra Park he would tuck my arm through his own. We made plans. How would they have turned out if we could have married? James returned from one of his trips and told me the only way I could stay in England was to marry a British man. To marry him. And why would I not do that? Had I not left my own home to marry James? Had I not betrayed my own papa to do as I pleased?

Life is so very difficult at times. What happened to my dreams? Did England suck them out of me like pips from pepper fruit? Or did I give them up and settle for what crumbs were thrown to me? James. It will be interesting to know if the runes have been thrown, to see where he can be buried. Oh, but I am thinking of him as an African. Mama was so disappointed when I married him. When finally I wrote to her, after many years, she told me to come home. Do not worry child, her letter said. Bring yourself home. But I could not.

'Ade, are you well?'

'Of course I am well, sister, why do you ask?'

'Well, we have driven over some of the most terrible roads and you have not complained once. I must think you are not feeling yourself.'

'Funmi, I will thank you to be thinking after your own health and leave mine to me, sha!'

'Mum don't be rude, she was only joking.'

'Hei! This Elizabeth of yours, she does not know you at all.'

'Shot down, Mum, haha. Hey Nan, it's like a hundred years since you was here last what's it feel like?'

'Can it be one hundred years, Kutes, when I am younger than Aunty Funmi and she is only eighty?'

'Yeah right, dunno how that works when you was seventeen when ya came to Manc an' you was born in like the 1920s.'

'Kutes! Don't speak to your grandmother like that.'

'Oh, chill out Mum I'm messing with her, jeez.'

This Kutes-o, she would have been my friend if we had been born together. She is fearless. How did my daughter manage to produce such a girl? Ah, but is she not like Olu, her grandfather?

'It's not funny, Mum, you just encourage her rudeness if you laugh at her.'

'Innit though, Nan, haha!'

My children have so much to learn. How can they learn a lifetime in one week?

'Funmi, what is this village? Look at the children running between the cars.'

'Do not buy any water from them, the water is not pure.'

'Yeah, I read that on lonely planet or summat, says you should only buy bottled water that's sealed.'

'There is a lonely planet-o? Well, it is not this one. This one has more than enough people going about it.'

'No aunty it's like a website, ya know, on the internet. It tells you about where you're going an stuff so you know what to do when you get there an you don't get mugged and ill and sh-stuff.'

'I did not hear one word of that child. It is a good job you have come home.'

'Whatever.'

'This is a very nice car Funmi, does it belong to you?'

'My son-in-law bought it for me and lends me his driver. It is useful but could make me old before I need to be.'

I do not have a son-in-law. I have missed too many things in my life.

I do have my old car but I am not able to drive it so well any more. Of course my daughter does not think I need one when she will go and do my shopping and drive me to the doctors and my hospital appointments. But in between, when I am sitting in my chair with nothing but television to keep me company I would like to have a son-in-law who thought that I needed a car and a driver.

'Hey Nan, when I pass me test in a few months I'll be your driver if you get me a car like this with air-con. I'll have a convertible.'

'Really child, and what will I buy this car with? Have we won the national lottery? Perhaps you think my pension benefits are so large I need an armed guard when I collect them.'

'Mum, you really shouldn't encourage her. You're acting just as bad. Kutes have some bloody manners.'

'Elizabeth! Chill out, sha!'

Elizabeth

I'm not going to Sapele. I'm staying in Benin. That's where my dad is. And I'm staying in a fucking hotel. With a generator. They can stay where they want. It looks dead outside. Everything's dry. And why's it so fucking hot if there's no sun?

'Kutes you keep poking me. Can't you move up a bit?'

'Whatever. What's them things at the side of the road?'

'Bushes, trees, shacks?'

'Tall mud things. Nan?'

'They are anthills. I had forgotten how they looked.'

'Cool.'

Anthills are cool? Is she mad? I refuse to get drawn into these senseless conversations. Why can't she just be quiet? Now we're driving into oncoming traffic. He's going to kill us.

I wonder where they've kept my dad's body. I hope they have a generator wherever it is or he'll be rotted before we bury him.

When I think about it, he didn't come back to see me for more than twenty years before he got ill. So really it was just about him. He didn't care about what I was doing. He didn't even know Kutes till she was grown up. And there's his other kids getting it all easy. It's not like I had a relationship with him. Flying visits with his stupid hat on. All loud voice and presents.

I was about six when he came in the summer time. I remember because he had short sleeves in his blue and white checked shirt. I was looking at his arms and he saw me and grabbed one of mine and put it next to his and told me he was darker than me. And he laughed. And everyone else in the room laughed, except Mum. And I didn't know why she wasn't laughing. But then she never did when he was around. Oh my god, I bet they weren't even married. No I'm being stupid of course they were married. I've seen the bloody marriage certificate.

God, I can't stand it in this car for much longer. But at least we're on the right side of the road. I hope we're going to stop somewhere soon.

'Are we going to stop for a break soon?'

'Yes daughter, can you see those buses parked up ahead? This is where we stop.'

They're not buses. I'm thirsty and I need the loo but I'm not going in a hole in the ground.

'Cool Mum, have you seen that. It's like Vegas or summat.'

'What are you talking about Kutes? It's a restaurant. You're going on like you've never seen one before.'

'Yeah, but it's like a proper one innit. Like KFC or summat and it's in the middle of all them wooden shacks and it's like desert and all dry and shit and then there's that an it's lit up sign.'

I give up on this girl. God, it's hot when the air con's off.

'Kutes will you hurry up and get out please.'

'Door dunt open.'

'Can somebody open the bloody door, please?'

'Elizabeth, sha. I think perhaps you need a cold drink to cool you down.'

'I needed to get out of the car, is all. Kutes will you come here.'

Ah, that's better, real air conditioning. And a signed toilet, inside the building.

'It's like Burger King or summat but with rice an yam. I'm starving. It smells wicked.'

'Kutes, I hardly think it can be like Burger King if it doesn't sell burgers. Go and see what you want, I'm just going to the loo.'

'Don't be friggin' hours you know what you're like.'

'Jeez Mum you've been friggin ages, I'm starving but they wouldn't let me eat till you got here and it's freezing in here and my food will be cold.'

'Don't exaggerate Kutes, I've only been a couple of minutes.'

Fried rice and chicken. I can do this.

'Elizabeth, is there something wrong with your food?'

'No, no, it's fine. I can't find my fork.'

'Duh, it's on the tray in front of you.'

'Yes Kutes, but that isn't mine, is it?'

She pulls a face at me. I ignore her. I don't want to be doing this. I'm staying in a hotel.

'Of course you are daughter. Ola has arranged it for you already. In New Benin.'

Damn, did I say that out loud or is Funmi reading my thoughts now?

'Really, Ola's done that?'

'Ade, has she also got hearing problems?'

'There's nothing wrong with my hearing, thanks, Aunt Funmi. I was just checking. You know, verifying.'

'Cool, we're staying in a hotel. Hope it's got internet.'

163

'Kutes, we did not come all the way here for you to sit in a room on the internet. You can do that at home.'

'I dint say I was sitting in me room did I, I only thought summat out loud. Jeez is there a law against that now?'

Kutes

for fucks sake

Ade

Hei! How will Elizabeth manage? My only one. Did I forget how long I waited for her? So many years. Even after Funmi wrote to me and told me of Papa's fate. Even after Mama wrote to me. For my shame I could not return to her.

'Ade? Are you with us? Perhaps the heat is too much?'

'Is it not strange how we each only had one daughter, and yet our own mamas had two?'

'This is what you are thinking?'

Hei, she is correct. I need to rest. There are too many memories.

'Nan, are you eating that chicken cos it's going cold an I'm still hungry.'

'Kutes, stop it, for god's sake.'

'Whatever.'

'Perhaps it is good that we each had only one daughter sha!'

Elizabeth

We're staying in a hotel. I should have known Ola would sort it out. He's a good kid really.

'Of course your mama will come home with me.'

'What? Mum, you're not staying at the hotel?'

'I have no business staying in hotels, Elizabeth. What for? I am home. Would you stay in the Midland if you were in Manchester?'

'How can I look after you if you're miles away? Don't be ridiculous, we're all staying in the hotel.'

'You see, Funmi. This is how it is. Suddenly I have become the child and she the adult.'

I can't stand it. I really can't stand it. When something happens to her it will be my fault.

'Cool, Nan. I'll still be able to come to where you are, innit. But I'm gonna stay with me mum in the hotel.'

'Of course child, you shall both come to Sapele tomorrow or next tomorrow.'

I can't be in the same room as Kutes. I really can't. But I can sort it out when we get there. I hope the hotel is all right. Ola wouldn't have booked me into somewhere bad, he must know I won't stay somewhere scruffy. He knew Dad better than me. I don't think I can do this. They'll all be telling me things about my dad and it's not fair. I don't know anything about the man. I can't go there and have them telling me things. I must know something that they don't. I knew his mum and stories about when he was growing up and things he got up to. Why didn't I listen properly? He grew up in a terraced house in Ardwick. I should have brought photos. There was one where he was about seven and in short pants and even though it's grainy you can see the scabs on his knees. And he was naughty. She said he would run around the streets and disappear and he was cheeky.

But how does any of that help? To me he was a sun-burned, wrinkled stranger. I was scared when he came home. He was loud and shouty and I hid under the table. He always had his feet pushed into leather sandals, or slippers as he called them. His hairy toes didn't reach the end and his cracked, dry heels would hang over at the back. I made maps out of the patterns on his feet. While he sat there and talked about Nigeria, I traced the patterns on his feet, never touching them, but almost. And he slid them in and out of his sandals when he got excited and I nearly got caught, touching. One time when he came, I don't remember how old I was, but I remember his big toenail was black and I thought he was turning into a black man.

'Elizabeth, are you not eating?'

'I didn't know my dad.'

Oh my god! What the hell is wrong with me? Don't look at them.

'I mean, I didn't know what he was like here, you know, living here with his family.'

'Yeah, well he dint know you either did he so what's the biggy.'

'Ade, you have very strange children. The driver is waiting.'

Who the hell is she to say we're strange? She thinks she has the right to comment and she doesn't even know us. I am not sitting in the middle this time, Kutes is smaller, she can go there. And I'm taking the damn child lock off.

'Kutes, get in next to your nan."

'Whatever.'

It can't be far now, we left Lagos over four hours ago. That's the first number I've thought about all day. And it wasn't even exact. Maybe I'm feeling better. Maybe everything's going to be ok. We'll stay in a clean hotel, we'll go to the funeral and then we'll be going home. Dia will be waiting at the airport and everything will go back to normal. I'll go back to normal.

'Does Ola know when we're arriving?'

'Yes, daughter, he will meet us at the hotel.'

You see, everything's going to be fine.

Kutes

Nigeria is fuckin awesome look at the size of this friggin bed an I can see the pool from here an the guy said theres internet fuckin awesome - whats this? no way theres even a little fridge and water in it an everythin - ewww don't like the bathroom much but theres soap an a proper shower wish carls was ere its gonna be so cool an that guy was well cute when we came in he looked a bit sweaty an that but its dead hot so no wonder an he was working - fuck me whos that fitty down there o shit hes got his girl with him - how comes all these guys here are cute yeah but in manc theyre all two toned crocodile skin shoes in puke brown an cream an trousers pulled up to their armpits and friggin ties an check shirts tucked in an here theyre all like casual hiphop shades ted baker t shirts and shit

'Wot?'

'Nothing I just thought I'd pop in and see if you're settling in.'

'Yeah, it's fine.'

'Well your nan's gone now, with aunty Funmi. To Sapele. And I don't know where Ola is. And I was thinking we could maybe have a walk around the hotel and...'

'Nah, I've got things to do.'

'Kutes? We're in a hotel in Nigeria. What possible things could you have to do?'

'Aww chill out, Mum wot ya goin on with I'm jus lookin round an sortin me stuff out, give me five yeah an I'll come to yer room an get ya.'

Shes fuckin bonkers no way is she gonna start with her fuckin stupidness when weve just got here for fucks sake Ola better get his arse here now an sort her out innit this is a chance in a lifetime like takin a year out an travellin only not with yer mates me an carls are sooo travellin next year we'll have a wikkid time cant wait - better go an get loopy tunes an have a walk round with her. It aint like me mum was born like that is it shes just fuckin stressed out an shit an she wont come out which is like mad yeah cos its 2008 an gays aint nothin well not nothing theyre like just people innit an nobody bothers bout it an me aunty dias cool - wish carly was here - no way theres summat wrong with me I always call her carls its bein round me cousins innit cos they all talk proper nah ill soon put a stop to that carls would be buzzin if she was here we'd be out on the street now checkin talent innit but instead ive gotta go and babysit me mum whos bonkers woohoo welcome to nigeria innit

Ade

I am unsure about leaving my daughters in this city. It has grown out of all proportion. What if they decide to go out? We should have warned them to stay indoors until we arrange a driver. But Ola will arrive shortly and all will be well.

This does not look like the country I left, with my grand ideas. And look at how I am living in Manchester compared to what I could have had if I had stayed. But what is happening to me? Will living on regrets make me happy?

'Ade, do not worry about your children, they will be fine. That is the best hotel and it is in New Benin and I have seen white men staying there.'

'I am not thinking about that. I am wondering about our village. Will I recognise anything?'

'Ade we live in a town now. Perhaps we will visit Ewuse if we have the time.'

Ewuse. I have not heard that name in such a long time.

'What of Amukpe? Is it still there?'

'You think perhaps somebody stole it? You have been away too long.'

Once my husband is buried I will be free. I would throw his body into the bush if it was left to me to arrange his funeral. Eh-heh! But what am I thinking? I have become a bitter old woman. I am a fool. I fell in love with a driver. He was a common driver. With golden hair and a smile that made me forget my name. How did I not know what could happen?

'Ade, what is it? I can feel your insides are not well.'

'No, sister, I am well. I am remembering and do not like it very much.'

'We will sit down together when we arrive and remember well-well.'

'Funmi, why are there blockades in the road? Is there a problem?'

'Ade, welcome to Delta State. This is what we say. You know that the oil refinery is in Warri, and we are heading towards Rivers. Our people think that we are all ready to steal some oil and become rich.'

'Well, why then is our driver handing over Naira? Is this how we live now?'

'Sister, you must not upset yourself like this. They are boys. Many have families to feed so they make what they can. It is nothing to spare twenty Naira.'

Pah! The country has gone mad. If one small boy had come to my father and asked for money simply to drive along a road he would have

170

beat him and he would have deserved it. There is no respect any more in my own country.

'Look, Ade. Welcome to Sapele. We are almost home.'

When we were children we would walk alongside the river to Sapele. Or sometimes if one of the boys in the village was carrying a load he would allow us to enter into his small boat. Yet now we are on a tarmac road.

'See here. Amukpe. It has changed, no?'

'Amukpe? This? how so? Was it not a village next to the river when I left?'

'Hah! Ade you are not the only person who has progressed. How would we drive in and out of Sapele if we did not have roads?

All these years I preserved the village in my mind like an old photograph.

Elizabeth

It's 5.30 and going dark and Kutes still hasn't come. Ola hasn't turned up and I need to put on some repellent because I don't want to be bitten. Why have they left me on my own?

Who's ringing me?

- Hello, hello? Dia is that you?
- Hey Beth, just a quick one. You ok, chick?
- I'm on my own.
- Where are you?
- In the hotel. Ola was supposed to meet us here. Kutes is in her room and she won't come and my mum's gone to Sapele.
- Oh, I thought you were lost in the middle of Lagos.
- But-
- Ring me when you get a sim card, this is costing you too much.
- Dia?

I can't believe she put the phone down on me. She can be such a bitch sometimes.

'Mum open the friggin door there's no air con out here.'

I open the door. Ola is standing next to Kutes.

'Where were you? You should have been here.'

'Sistah. I am so sorry. It was my mum, she was feeling sick.'

'Oh, jeez, Mum, I can't believe you've been bleaching. You're on holiday for god's sake. Can't you give it a rest? Oh shit, don't cry. Ola do something.'

'Sistah, it is fine.'

'I'm not crying.'

It's all so easy for them because they're young. They won't always be. How can they understand what I'm feeling?

Edema is here with the car. Let us go out now to eat. Is that ok?

'Cool I'm starvin. Where we goin?'

She's got no fear this daughter of mine.

'I'm coming. You can wait for me downstairs. I'll be down in a few minutes.'

I'm not going out with them. I didn't come here to enjoy myself.

'Mum, we're waiting, what ya doin?'

'I have a headache. I'm going to lie down. You go ahead.'

'Whatever.'

172

She's so rude. I was only ever like that once, when Dad came home. I was about twelve. There was a netball tournament after school. We'd been practising for weeks and then on the day my mum said I had to be home on time because my dad was coming. I was hysterical. It was the tournament and I was sure I'd told her about it. There was no way I was going to miss it. She slapped me. Hard. I ran out without my coat all the way to school. And in registration I was called out to the office and my mum was there with my coat and lunch. And my P.E. kit. She just hugged me and said 'play well, Elizabeth'.

Later they were both in the crowd of parents watching. I was embarrassed. They looked so different and I just wanted normal parents like everybody else.

'What?'

'Sistah, it is me, Ola. Come out with us. We will eat.'

'I have a headache.'

'Do you need some tablets? Will I get you some water?'

'No.'

'Ok, sis, I will bring you some chicken and rice.'

I should lock the door.

'Ya know what Mum, yer better stop it, yeah cos I'm gonna tell me Aunty Dia. Yer acting like a kid innit.'

'Get out.'

'Nah yer out of order. Everyone's bein dead nice and yer spoilin it for everyone.'

'Who do you think you're talking to? I'm not one of your friends.'

'Dead right cos they wouldn't carry on like this. I'm friggin sick of it now.'

I can't believe my own daughter can stand there and talk to me like that. She's had a better life than I did. I didn't shove her to one side and run meetings and have people around all the time. Where're my pyjamas?

Kutes

'Innit though Ola, shes well out ov order it aint like its anyones fault yer dad died an it aint even as though he was only her dad shes off her head an I aint putting up with it all week yeah like as though noone else has got a life an it aint like shes perfect or anything but its all about her id rather be with me nan than stayin in the next room to that an theres no way Im goin to the friggin funeral cos she'll just make it all about her and shes a fuckin hypocrite anyways cos its not like she let me know my dad its like whenever I used to mention it shed have to take to her bed and then clean like a fucker as though it was a dirty word its like she thinks she found me in a cabbage patch or summat but if she carries on yeah I'm gonna drop some lyrics on her about my dad she wont like that but I swear down I will it aint all about her'

Ade

'Ade, will you eat now?'

'No, Funmi. I am tired-o. I will rest.'

What did I expect to find here? And I have abandoned my daughters in that big city. What was I thinking? I should have stayed with them. They know nothing of this country, Elizabeth will become ill, Kutes will run around in the streets and be in danger. I am not a good mother.

Look at this big house that Funmi lives in. It is beautiful with its marble floors and leather chairs that I do not even think have been sat in ever. Funmi, who did not have a home when we were growing up, now lives like a queen. And I live in one room sitting in a chair, with children who force themselves to knock on my door and visit with me once a week if I am lucky.

These are the choices I made. I travelled with James but I was very much in love with Olu. Why did I hesitate? But I did not deserve happiness. I was a stupid girl. A stupid, silly girl.

The first time Olu asked me to marry him for real my heart stood still as though I was facing a wild boar in the bush and dare not move. I had not known him for more than two years and he was completing his first course at the university. He asked me to leave James, sell my house and go to live with him in London. But I hesitated. My heart shouted yes, but I could not abandon my house and the students who came and boarded with me. What would happen to them? My students sat around my table and ate properly, belonged to a family, did not have to worry about a landlord who would call them boy or worse. No, I could not leave my house at that time.

Olu understood. He said he would wait for me. He did too. For five years he travelled regularly to visit me. I even went to the capital once. The journey was long and tiresome and the boarding house he had booked me was neither pleasant nor clean. My clothes appeared out of place amongst those young women who dressed up simply to go to the market. I did not understand how Olu could want to be with me when he was surrounded with so many choices. We argued. I argued. He told me plainly that I was being silly. I had been saving every kobo I could from my boarders and the jobs I did. But, of course, I had to send money home regularly.

Always there was James and his meetings and his visitors that he would bring to the house and expect me to feed and give a free bed to.

There were even times over the summer months when I would have a house full of James's comrades, or so he called them, and I would have to use my savings to feed them. Why did I not say no?

So I remained. I could not marry my Olu when he came to me qualified as a lawyer and ready to return home. I was again pregnant with James's child. Another one that I lost. It was my punishment. Even though Olu did not know about what we had done, he should have understood that as the eldest daughter I had a duty to return home with more than I had left. So Olu left me and five years later Funmi told me of his marriage.

It was many years later that Elizabeth was born and James decided that we would return to Nigeria. By that time he made me sick to look at him. He did not understand what I was capable of and the one time he raised his hand to strike me I screamed so loudly my students came running to the kitchen. They stood around me, saying nothing, and he was forced to turn and walk through the door. Elizabeth, such a good baby, had slept through it all.

Of course, he returned later that evening and acted as though nothing had happened. I served him pepper soup, extra hot, and retired to my bedroom with the baby, locking the door behind us.

Funmi had written to me of all that was happening in Nigeria. The British were not about to hand back a country that had supplied them with so much and more. There would be a fight and I did not intend to take my daughter into that.

Today I will rest and tomorrow we will make arrangements to see the family and maybe Olu. Ah! Olu. I wonder how he is doing. It will be interesting to see how he is living. I am sure he is a big man in Warri.

'Ade, are you resting well?'

'Yes. Will I come through now? Although I would like to bathe first.'

'Have you been crying? Hah! It is too painful to return home, is it not? You should not have left us for so long.'

'Funmi, you open your mouth and it is full of dust as usual. Did you not learn any wisdom with all the years you have carried?'

'Hei, it is good to have you home. I have missed my only true sistah.'

'Well perhaps you could send me some water to bathe as you have missed me so much.'

And I have missed Funmi, though she does not need to hear this, it will only make her head swell.

'You do not change, Ade. I know you are pleased to be home. Perhaps you will stay here with me now, so that we can grow old together.'

'And what of my children? I am just to abandon them to England? You have seen how Elizabeth is and Kutes cannot even speak properly. What kind of mother would I be to leave them so?'

'They are adults now. Can you not find a man to look after them?'

'Hah! Please. They would lock you up for even thinking that way. Besides I did not have a man to look after me and I am fine.'

'Ade, you are British, sha!'

'And you are as stupid as you have always been.'

Elizabeth

Mum wants us to go to Sapele, but the roads aren't all that safe and the hotel is nice enough. It gets quite lively in the evenings down by the pool. I could be in Portugal on the Algarve when the music starts. I haven't been down because they're all young and dressed up like it's a club night, but I like watching from the window. The pool is all lit up and couples are sitting at tables, groups of guys are eyeing up groups of girls. And the music is exactly the same as the stuff Kutes listens to. Retro, house music, and then some remixes of the classics Dia and I danced to, and in between there's random African rap music and the guys go wild and show off some moves. It's literally like being on holiday and it's comforting and surreal at the same time. I'm sure I saw Kutes down there last night but I couldn't be sure. If she was, she blended in just fine, which means I don't need to worry so much, I guess.

Ola's been really good, and Edema, driving Kutes all over. She's been raving about markets and carving shops and Chicken Republic, which is apparently the KFC of Nigeria. She's telling me the rules about what to drink from the street vendors and not to get on the ocadas. It's funny that she's picking up words here so easily yet she struggles to speak proper English. At least I don't have to worry about her getting on the back of a motorbike, she listens to Ola.

If we go to Sapele, I don't know what Kutes will think about it. No fast food places. No trendy young people. Her nan's there on her own. We should have all stayed together.

I don't think Ola's sisters like me. They look at me strangely, hardly talk to me, just grin and look at each other. I can't stand it. It's not like I asked them to come to the hotel. They have kids, seven or eight between them. It's not like they're Catholic. Although maybe they are. My dad could have been a bloody Catholic. Why don't I know that? They might do a mass at his funeral. Shit. Oh, no, of course he wasn't. He was communist. Jeez, I need to go out today. I need to see people and do something before I go mad.

Kutes

I seriously don't think I can stand another few days here with her. She goes on like I'm selfish. Yeah right. I'm so telling me Aunty Dia when we get back. Me nan used to take me with her when I was little and me mum had one of her effing turns yeah. I bet she was well out raving when we was away. I wanna go an see me nan now I've had enough.

At least Ola and his mate take me downstairs to the pool at night. It's proper buzzing. And I can drink and shit. It's a good job I listened to Carls and put some proper clothes in me case. It's like all disco lights and rap music, I swear. I was recording it and these guys were doing a sick dance with foot flicks and the lot. Carls is gonna piss her sides when I send it.

And then before when I was getting ready Carls was telling me Wahidas probably got her stay which is fucking awesome and we did that cos we're shit hot. They're well gonna be celebrating but we'll have to do it again when I get home innit. I'm not missing out.

Ade

It is time those children of mine came now. It has been two days. I will send one of Funmi's children to bring them. Maybe I need to travel back to Benin, hei, but my body is tired.

How would my life have become had I returned? I look at all that Funmi has achieved. Am I wrong to think like that? No, at my age I can think how I please.

'Ma, Mummy says you have one visitor and you must fix yourself properly. Will I get you some water?'

'Child, do not tell me one visitor, is it not somebody with a name?'

'Mummy says she will beat me sore if I say anything else.'

'Pah, she is living in the dark ages. Tell her I am coming.'

He is quite a cute child. I do not know if he is Funmi's grandchild or great grandchild. The only boy I have seen in our family. I have missed out on so many years. This heat is far too much for a person to deal with. Was it always so hot? Or is climate change also affecting my country? Sha! What am I thinking? I have a visitor and I will go and greet him. It must be Olu. Why else would I not be told who had come?

I am feeling like a small child at Christmas and yet I am not moving from this chair. I do not believe I am ready to visit with him yet. What will he see when he looks at me. I was so lively when I was young. Life had so much promise. And I did nothing. But there is no reason for me to think like that now. Are we not both closer to the end of our lives than the beginning? Now, which wrapper will I wear? Or perhaps I should put on my cotton trouser and a nice blouse. Hah! I am like a small girl going on her first date. What does it matter how I dress? I will put on my green and blue wrapper. This way he may not notice how I have changed in my shape.

'Ade, did I not send Ebi to fetch you one hour ago?'

'Funmi, I am coming. I do not move as fast as I once did.'

'Well soon our visitor will leave and believe we have no manners in this house. Are you set?'

'Would you have me greet somebody when I am not ready?'

Funmi talks like my mama, her voice carries the exact inflection. And she moves her hand just so when she is agitated. She is more Mama's daughter than I am. But now I will go and greet my past.

This passageway is dark. The house has not been built well to utilise the light from outside. Hei! I think I may be turning into my daughter with these ridiculous thoughts that creep into my mind. That's better, now I can see. I cannot hear any voices, they must be in the front room. Oh! Who is this now?

'Ade, this is Ola's mama. She has travelled to meet with you.'

Why is Funmi looking at me like that? Does she think I have no manners?

'Good afternoon, how are you?'

'Ahhh, wife! I am too sad. Is it not a terrible matter?'

Why is this woman here? She looks anything but sad to me with her stiff headpiece and gold-flecked wrapper. And I do believe I recognise those earrings she has in her long earlobes. They belonged to my mama I am sure. That man stole them. She has come to brag to me.

'How, now, MamaTosan, are you well?'

'Yes wife, I am as well as I can be. I heard from my children that you had travelled and I know that our husband would want me to greet you.'

This is unbearable and Funmi can stop pulling that face at me. I do not need to associate myself with this woman.

'Yes, my daughter wished to attend her papa's funeral and I did not wish for her to travel alone. You know how some of our people behave.'

She looks old and fat. And her eyes are bad, I can tell by how she is squinting. She must not go near to my daughters. This woman is wicked. Does she not know custom? Even I have not forgotten that wives do not meet or attend the husband's funeral. Have circumstances changed so much or is it because she was married to a white man? I know that Funmi does not like this woman so why is she bringing her into her home?

'Funmi, will you arrange some food for MamaTosan before she leaves. I need to lie down the heat is too much!'

Look at her fat lips trying not to smile. She believes that she is better than me. She is welcome to the role of widow. I will not stand in her way.

'Wait, Ade, your children have arrived. Will you not wait until they come?'

'No Funmi, you can send them to me.'

Look at her. I would slap her if I was ten years younger. But Funmi is right. I cannot leave my children to face her alone. I have not forgotten the things she said to my Elizabeth, that wicked-wicked woman. Let her see how my child has grown and has one daughter of her own. Hah!

'Perhaps you could turn on the generator Funmi, so that we may have air conditioning for a small while?'

'So MamaTosan, how are your children? Are they well?'

'Not so well, wife. You know that we have very little now that our husband has gone. It is so sad. Too sad. And our youngest daughter has not yet completed school and I do not know where we will find the fees.'

Perhaps I did not hear the old witch correctly. No, I must not have done. She cannot possibly be asking me to pay for her children-sha!

'Oh dear, I am sure your children will do well. Ola is doing very fine at his studies I believe and he has been living well in my daughter's house. Perhaps it is time your own daughter married and had a husband to care for you. I am sure your youngest must now be 28 years.'

'Ah, but she wishes to be a doctor. Does this not take many years? It was her papa's wish that she should study medicine.'

As if that useless man had one thought running through his head that did not concern politics and what he could get out of his status. Pah! I will not even answer her. Where are my children?

'Well if that is what her papa wished for her he will have provided I am sure. If not perhaps you will go and find work as I did for my own daughter. There is always a way forward, is there not?'

Hah! That wiped the smile from her face.

'Mum, are you ok? You don't look very well.'

'Ah Elizabeth, are you well, daughter? This is Ola's mama. I think she may be leaving soon.'

'Errmm, yes, hello. I didn't expect to see you here. We meant to come and visit you, but Ola said you weren't very well.'

A-ha! My daughter has good manners, 'Perhaps if you are not feeling well you should go home now.'

How dare she snub my children?

'Do you need anything from us for the funeral? It is on Friday, is it not? Will I give you some more money for food, or perhaps decoration?'

'No wife, we have everything arranged. It will be a small funeral as our husband requested. Everything has been put in place and the grave has been dug at the bottom of the compound. We will not take him into the house. You will discuss with Ola about your contribution.'

The cheek of this woman. Have we not contributed enough already? So this is how it will be for James, the great 'I am'. He will be buried by the compound wall. I do not believe it is his request. I imagine that she has gone and thrown the runes and could not bury him in a sacred place. I will not mock and I will not give her one kobo more than we have already paid. The useless man left nothing for his family, but that is not my concern. Did I not struggle all of those years while she was walking around in my mama's earrings?

'Okay then, goodbye and thank you for taking the trouble to call. We shall see you before we leave I am sure.'

'Oh, when will you leave Adeola? When will you travel?'

Hei! So now she can use my name, instead of calling me wife? What kind of woman is this?

'Next two weeks. Do not worry we will be staying for some time. Kutes do not interrupt when I am speaking. Go to the kitchen and see if aunty needs some help.'

As if I will tell this witch the date we are leaving so that she can put bush-craft on us. I do not think so.

Elizabeth

Mum's acting strange. I don't know what's wrong with her. She keeps looking at me as though I've got two heads. I've only been here for an hour. Kutes isn't speaking to me. I can't stand it. I have a headache.

Kutes

Shit, me Aunty Funmi's house is well cool. It's massive and proper posh with its leather sofas. I'm gonna have cream leather sofas when I get me own flat after travelling of course. I might share with carls. Oh my god look at the size of that friggin cooker hob its got at least 8 burners thought they dint have gas. No way its run on calor gas like a massive camping stove – cool

'Me nan says Ola's mums goin so I should come and tell you and she said summat about we ain't leaving for 2 weeks. Wot's she going on about, fem?'

Oh shit, did I swear. What's she looking at me like that for. Nah I'm sure I didn't and why's me mum laughing? Oh, I get it she didn't understand me yeah well whatever at least me mums cracking her face instead of pulling it.

I'm gonna find Ola and Edema at least I can have a laugh with them. It's like starting again every time I go to a new house and they don't understand me. That's their problem innit and look at the size of that bedroom and the bed. It's bigger than the one in the hotel and the wardrobes well posh with all that lacquer but only if ya like that sort of thing maybe I can stay here for a bit, beats goin to a friggin funeral.

Ade

I cannot believe Funmi allowed that woman to come into her home. Does she not remember what she is capable of? This is what made my daughter like she is. Funmi herself protected Elizabeth.

'Sister, is it not true that you kept my daughter safe from that same woman who was sat here?'

'What is this now, Ade? The woman came to show respect.'

'Pah, she came to see what she could get.'

Maybe I am not remembering correctly, it was a long time ago.

'Did Elizabeth not come to you when this woman tried to harm her?'

'Ade, the woman has problems with her mind sometimes, but she lost so many babies when she was younger. You know how the women love to gossip and say it is for this reason or that reason. The fact that she was married to a white man who already had a child was a good story for those witches to enjoy.'

'But Elizabeth was so ill when she returned home. You yourself had told her that she was in danger from juju.'

'Hei, Ade, you are tiring me now. You want me to remember something that happened twenty years ago? Our daughter was upset and her papa was not any use. Maybe I told her one thing or another to make her see sense and go home. It was not safe. The country was in turmoil. We did not want her to be roaming around Delta State alone and you know how strong willed that child was.'

'I am too tired to argue with you. I will go and rest.'

I cannot tell if Funmi is remembering wrong of if it is my own memory that fails me. But it is true that it was long ago and Elizabeth was always an anxious child.

'Ade, your daughter is very much like you, is she not? What of the stories about my own mama? Do you not remember how we would scare each other so much that we became afraid to go into the bush? But my mama was sick also.'

'Hei, Funmi, do not begin with that now. Your mama was wicked and you know so. Did she not beat me when I was a small child? Did she not put curses on my own head?'

'Well, she was not very good at cursing then because you have had a fine life in London.'

'Is it so, sister? You have no idea.'

'Do you not remember your own words to that man? Was it not of your own making that your papa was arrested and your mama left to fend alone?'

'Why you dey bring am up now o? Have I not suffered enough?'

'Woah, Nan, chill, wots up? No way are you arguing.'

'Is this what I came for, Funmi? For you to tell my children of my wickedness. Is this what you have waited for all these years? Even now the man will not let me be.'

'Still you are the same, Ade. Everyone is doing to you. Am I telling lies? Did you not convince the man that he would die by your papa's hand if he did not marry you?'

'And do you not think that every day I have lived with this knowledge? Did I know that he would report my papa?'

'Mum, what's going on? Kutes go and get some water.'

'Funmi has decided it is well for me to remember my past sins. Perhaps I should flog myself in the village square.'

'I am teaching you compassion. You seem to forget that love can turn a person's head, is it not?'

I did nothing wrong. It was that man, James. I did not know for many years what he had done. I tried to make it up. I sent money. Funmi is so sure of herself and what she believes in. England has turned my own head inside out. I stayed away too long. No amount of letters could make up. I messed up big time. That is how Kutes would say it.

'Ade, are you well, sister?'

'Can we change the past, sister? If we could I would not have told James my papa would kill him if he left me here pregnant. If it were not for those fateful words our destinies would have been very different.'

'Ade you have become a philosopher. Perhaps you should write a book.'

'When I left my mama for that man and he betrayed my papa to his bosses so that he did not have to face him – that was when my story was written.'

'Adeola, water wey person go drink, nor fit pass am by.'

'Hei. Perhaps it is so.'

Elizabeth

The funeral is tomorrow and we're still in Sapele. Just sitting and listening to Mum and Aunty Funmi talk has made so much sense of so many things. All these years I've thought Ola's mum cursed me and all along it was just me being me and my dad acting weird because of his own stuff. It's like I've been given the crayons to colour in between the lines. All this time I've felt as though I'm not real, as though I couldn't match up to Mum or Dad. As though I was outside the Nigeria club. All that time. What a waste.

Does everyone live pretend lives? They must. Dad pretended to be African. Mum pretended to be British. Maybe they weren't pretending though. I was. I was pretending to be straight. I'm not pretending anymore. I'm so lucky Dia is still around. I know she's seen other people over the years. But she's always been around. What if I'd been as brave as her after all those rallies we went to in the 70s. That's when Dia stood up and decided who she was and what she was. It was so different then. I couldn't turn round to my mum and say, hey I'm a lesbian feminist. A Black British feminist. I couldn't because I didn't feel black. And I didn't feel like a feminist. And I wanted to be normal.

'Aunty says you should come and eat.'

'I'm not hungry.'

'She says you've got to whether you're hungry or not.'

'Okay.'

Why's she still standing there? That's the most she's said to me in two days. I should say something but I don't know what.

'Kutes, I'm sorry.'

'You was out of order, Mum. It ain't like any of this is my fault.'

'I said I'm sorry. I'll be there in a bit.'

She has to push it. I don't know why I bothered.

I don't want anything to eat. I like being outside though. Down here by the river it's shaded by trees and it's so peaceful. I feel like nothing matters. Maybe it's Funmi – so calm and matter of fact. I haven't even counted since I got here. Each time I start to get stressed she knows and gives me something to do.

There's nothing left of my mum's village. A few old stones and a big tree were all that I saw. I thought my mum was going to cry. But Funmi was right, you don't need a small, old village when you've got a town. No electricity, no running water. Funmi says she wouldn't swap her washing machine for the riverbanks.

Four more days then we're going home. Dia will be waiting for me. I hope I don't have to see Ola's mum again. She still scares me. The river's so wide and blue. I think I could sit by it forever. I'd like to take it home with me. Or maybe bring Dia here. God I'm missing her.

Kutes

Na wah oh! I can't believe me nan was arguing like that with aunty, but I suppose it's like sisters or summat innit. I felt well sorry for me nan cos it's like when you do summat and then you think no one remembers and it's just you then you wake up in the night an yer hearts racing cos you think you're gonna be found out. Damn me nan must have been like that for years.

When I went into her room she was just lying there and looking proper sad so I told her stuff about Emre and how I was using him for lifts and shit and that it's just wot happens innit cos I wanted her to feel better but it didn't really make any difference so I just held her hand and then Funmi comes and tells me to get me mum but I think she was gonna make me nan feel better cos at the end of the day it ain't me nans fault if he got her preggers and I bet he made her feel guilty forever which is why she stuck with him. He was well out of order, anyways.

At least we don't have to go to the funeral now I feel a bit sorry for Ola innit but not sorry enough to go with him anyways me nan says I shouldn't so that's cool. We don't want no more wahallah me aunty says.

It's a bit dead here I wanna go back to Benin or go somewhere else. I hope Edema and Ola are coming today. They said they would so I can at least go for a drive with them somewhere. It was so boring yesterday we had to go down a dirt track and past broke down old houses to find a village that doesn't exist anymore. And me mum's like 'oooh, ahhhh' look at that and me nan's acting like everything should still be the same as like a hundred years ago, as if.

Aunty Funmi's ok I suppose but she's a bit full on dunt miss a trick and she keeps telling me bout how I'm talking which is a bit of a joke when I can't even catch what she's saying half the time. The house is pretty cool though I like the marble on the floors and I like the way there's balconies but dunno why they're all covered up with that lattice stuff. I need to go to an internet caff and chat with carls she'll think I've been abducted innit. I'll tell her about all the Naija boys but I need to get some pics with some to make her well jel.

I'm sick of people coming to look at us like we're in a zoo or summat cos about ten thousand people've come and said they're cousin of this and that and I swear they can't all be related specially as me nan only had one sister and me Aunty Funmi only had one sister so how many peeps can

190

be family?

Ade

Funmi believes she is clever, telling me which wrapper to wear today and sending the girl to braid my hair. She thinks I do not know what she is planning. I will not spoil her surprise. Today I am sure I will visit Olu. After all these years I will look at him again. Funmi tells me he did not remarry, but I do not believe he is alone.

Ah-ha! I can see a car. I am sure any moment now she will come and fetch me and we will go. If I lived here, I would spend most of my time sitting on this balcony. There is a breeze coming through the grill at the far end and it keeps me cool. And out through this side I can glimpse the river and I am sure that is my mama's tree. Right over there. Of course it is blurred but I do not wish to go inside for my glasses. I will ask Funmi when she comes.

Mama's tree. The place of the secret women's meetings, hah! That was many lifetimes ago. What would she think of me now, my mama? How would my life have been if I had stayed with her? I would be sitting on my own balcony just like this one, enjoying a cool morning breeze. Perhaps I should have stayed.

'Ade, is it you?'

'Olu? But why are you here?'

'Ah, that is my Ade! Still you have not learned to think before you open your mouth.'

But this is an old man. If I only heard his voice I would not doubt that this is my Olu; his hair is so white-o. Does he think that silly hat will hide it? Olu and his hats. I remember the first time I saw him.

'Ade, can you not greet me. Perhaps the shock is too great for your old heart!'

'Don't be so cheeky. Olu-sha! It is good to see you, please come and sit. Talk to me. It has been so long. Too long.'

Elizabeth

This spot by the river has become my place. I was so relieved that we didn't have to go to the funeral. Even Ola told us not to. How the hell could it take so long for them to decide he wasn't getting a proper funeral? Mum thinks it was a way of getting money from us, that they were never going to bury him properly. I don't feel bad.

'Elizabeth? Is it you?'

'I'm sorry. Do I know you? You shouldn't sneak up on people like that.'

'Elizabeth, it is me. I came to offer my condolences for your loss. And perhaps to meet my daughter again.'

Oh my god, oh my god. One two three four five six seven eight nine ten. What's he doing here? Oh fuck, fuck, fuck. What am I going to say? I feel sick.

'Elizabeth, are you ok? Will I get you some water?'

'No. I'm fine. I'm fine. What are you doing here? Why the hell are you here?'

'I travelled with my papa. He is not able to drive so easily now. He did not tell me you were here. Aunty sent me to you.'

Meddling old bag. What's she playing at? And there's me thinking she was ok. This is what happens. You let your guard down for a second and bam!

'I don't know what you mean.'

'Elizabeth, is it not true that we had a baby?'

'Kutes doesn't need a dad, she's fine.'

'Still. Perhaps she will like to meet me.'

I think I'm having a heart attack. This isn't supposed to happen. I obviously wanted a baby, but I didn't want him. Not later anyway. I knew I was going to be with Dia, I was waiting. She'd been my best friend and I'd been there when she split up with that girl she was in love with. And I was waiting till she was over her. I'd planned a night for us and there'd only been two weeks to go and she'd be ready for a new relationship. I don't even know where I got that information. The exact time it takes to get over a broken love affair, obviously some crappy magazine. Then he turned up on the doorstep wanting to see me again. But he didn't know about Kutes. And Dia didn't know how I felt about her. Everything was a mess. I had to tell him in the end and I let him hold her but he was scared you could tell and we agreed that I wouldn't say anything as long as he left us alone.

'You promised, Femi. Why are you doing this?'

'Please Elizabeth. Don't cry. Perhaps it will be for the best. You've brought Kutes home. Maybe in your mind you wanted this to happen. '

Did I? That's news to me. Kutes doesn't know anything. She didn't need to know. Oh shit, I don't know. I want Dia to be here. She'd know what to do. No, actually, Dia would be laughing with him by now and playing remember-when, not squirming on a rock and feeling like shit. Kutes will never speak to me again. I don't even know what the last story was that I told her about her dad. Shit, shit, shit. He can't meet her here. Not at my spot by the river. He can meet her somewhere else. Hell, what am I talking about? My spot? It's not like I'm ever coming back here.

'I don't know what to do. You promised to stay away. You won't even understand her.'

'Haha! You are still funny Elizabeth. I lived in Birmingham for ten years after I graduated. I understood that accent very well, so I am sure I will understand my own daughter.'

'Oh my god, she's coming. Shit.'

Kutes

Na bloody Wah OOOO!

So, yeah, I'm chillin with Ola an me Aunty Funmi yeah she calls me in an tells me I've got a visitor like der!!! Who the fuck knows me out here? But she like insists and sends me out to the river and it's like I can imagine being born here an being sent to the river for woteva, yeah, woteva they used to send kids to the river for.

My mum's down there and I can tell from the back door that she's got one on her and there's this guy talking to her and I swear its like I know him or summat but I can only see him from the side so I reckon its like Edema's brother or dad or summat cos I don't know anyone else here. So I goes down the garden and then me mum sees me and she looks like she's seen a ghost or summat and the guy turns round and smiles at me and it's a bit creepy cos I swear I know him. Then, fuck me if me mum don't grab hold of me like I'm a kid and then she's like mumbling shit so I thought she was having a stroke or summat.

It's only me fucking dad. I swear down, it's like no fucking way, it's my dad. All this time she ain't told me nothing about him and then he's there stood right in front of me and I didn't have anything to say.

I felt a bit sorry for me mum cos its like she was scared or summat, but fuck me I've got a fuckin dad hahahahahahahaha! And it's like mad, yeah, and he's dead smart and he aint got any other kids which is like cool cos he owes me for nearly 18 years so its better for him if he aint got other kids innit. I need a car and that's what dads are supposed to do. Course, I cant just ask him outright I'll have to wait for a bit and get to know him and all that.

Eh-eh! It's like a fucking story. I aint being selfish or nothing but I want my dad to myself and I know me mum's a lezzer, yeah, but obviously she weren't always else I wouldn't be here would I? I feel like I could throw up but I don't know if it's cos I'm happy or sick. I've got a dad, yeah, and a new grandad who's me nan's friend so it's like incest or summat hahahahahaha! It's cool cos he's like a proper old gentleman and me nan goes all soft and shit when she's near him and I think she's gonna stay with him but she might not cos I don't think I'd like it if my nan wasn't downstairs cos shes always there.

Ade

I am happy. I did not believe it could be possible to feel like this once more.

Elizabeth

-Dia, it's me.
    -About time too, what the hell's been going on?
    -You wouldn't believe me if I told you.
    -Hurry up home, Beth, I'm missing you.
    -Me too. Dia?
    'Yeah?'
    -I love you. Will you move in with me?
    -What?
    -When I come back. Will you move in with me?
    -Finally you've grown up. I'm waiting.